CW00518245

Frances Harrison Marr

Heart-life in Song

Frances Harrison Marr

Heart-life in Song

Reprint of the original, first published in 1883.

1st Edition 2024 | ISBN: 978-3-38531-606-5

Verlag (Publisher): Outlook Verlag GmbH, Zeilweg 44, 60439 Frankfurt, Deutschland
Vertretungsberechtigt (Authorized to represent): E. Roepke, Zeilweg 44, 60439 Frankfurt, Deutschland
Druck (Print): Books on Demand GmbH, In de Tarpen 42, 22848 Norderstedt, Deutschland

HEART-LIFE IN SONG,

BY

MISS FANNIE H. MARR.

Know'st thou a noble action?—Tell it wide,
That fainter hearts may learn to do or bear.
Hast thou a worthy thought?— Clothe it with words,
And it may live when thou hast passed away.

SECOND EDITION.

RICHMOND, VA.:
J. W. RANDOLPH & ENGLISH AND WEST, JOHNSTON & CO.
1883.

CONTENTS.

HEART LIFE IN SONG.

KOSHAGAUTAMI.

A HINDOO LEGEND.

WHEN Time was young, and Buddha dwelt
    with men,
Uttering his precious words of wisdom; when
The wronged, the suffering, and the needy came
To ask his counsel, or his aid to claim,
It chanced that by him often-times there stood
A simple, artless daughter of the wood,—
Koshagautami,—who, with eager ear
And timid heart, like graceful fawn, drew near,
Listened awhile, then lightly disappeared,
As if observing eye she shunned and feared.
Often had Buddha watched her standing by,
With glowing, parted lips, and kindling eye;
But when he sought, with prophet glance, to see
Her inner, hidden life,—then, even he,

  2

Buddha, so great, and wise, and learnéd styled,
Was baffled, thwarted, by the woman-child.

With all the buoyant hope and trust of wife,
She, with her chosen, was just entering life.
Far from the haunts of men, the happy two
Lived for each other, faithful, kind and true.
Rich in the treasure of a priceless love,
Guileless and peaceful as the gentle dove,
Their present flowed too smoothly, swiftly on
To leave one sigh for days or pleasures gone;
And to their gaze the future only cast
A brightened image of the happy past.

One little boy made short the long, glad days
With cooing laughter and sweet, childish ways,
And won, without an effort, without art,
The wild, deep worship of the mother's heart.
She loved,—but not as we of colder climes,
Of calculating days and reasoning times,
Who give, despite of Nature's loud demand,
A measured love, with cautious heart and hand.
Her love—a full, deep current—strongly flowed
With every beat of pulse, and stream of blood—

Intensified existence—calmed its strife,
And was her food, her air, her breath, her life.

One day the prattle ceased; the laughter fled;
The little limbs grew still;—the child was dead.
The wondering mother fondly, wildly pressed
The cold, stiff infant to her throbbing breast.
She rocked and shook him; then she sang and cooed;
Then forced between his lips the savory food;
Then rubbed and chafed him; tossed him to and fro;
For oh! the heavy silence awed her so,
She would have leaped with joy to hear again
That infant voice, although in moans of pain!
Alas! where had the artless mother been
Ne'er to have known the penalty of sin?
Ne'er to have known the chill, the vanished breath,
The awful stillness of what we call—death?

With love that never curbs her strong desires;—
With love that never falters, never tires;
With love that never yields to cold despair,
But wills and acts, though Reason says, "Forbear;"—
Koshagautami placed the lifeless form
Upon her hips, and on, through sun and storm,

Wandered o'er plains, and up and down the wood,
Asking each passer what would do him good.
And all, with innate courtesy, gave place,
Looked pityingly into the wistful face
And hollow eyes that asked so strange a thing,
Yet never help or ray of hope could bring;
And then the patient mother thought of one
To whom all things were easy, all things known;
And with a new strong hope she turned with haste
To seek the aid of India's mighty Priest.
"Surely," she said, stilling her bosom's woes,
"Surely some help, some hope, great Buddha knows."

He sat beneath a spreading banyan tree,
And men had gathered all around, while he
Unfolded to them from the mighty deep
Of his own soul some thought, some truth, to keep.
O Buddha, when, like mountain capp'd with snows,
Above the plain of common minds thou rose,
Seeking, with only Nature's light and lore,
To make men wiser, better than before,
Thou sought the noblest task that e'er was given
To fallen man by an o'er-ruling heaven!
And if in darkness thou didst blindly grope,

Striving in vain the close-barred gates to ope
That swelled the tide of ignorance and doubt,
And shut the floods of higher knowledge out,
Thy soaring spirit in its daring flight,
Caught now and then a glimmer of the light!

The truly great are good, and when he saw
Koshagautami gently near him draw,
And read upon her young and clouded face
The lines that only spirit grief can trace,
His heart, with tender, soothing pity stirred,
And his kind ear waited her opening word.

How strong and brave love makes us! Ne'er before,
Save in the distance humbly to adore,
Had she dared gaze on him; yet now, without
One check of fear, one shade of blinding doubt,
Or thought of aught, save that she came to crave,
And that he held the power to help and save;
She came—the lifeless burden on her hips;
She came—the heart-wish trembling on her lips.

"Behold," said she, "my child! How still he lies!
How cold and stiff his limbs! How strange his eyes!

Vainly I've tried each simple charm and art;
No word, no laughter comes to cheer my heart.
But dost not thou, O blessed Master, know
Something to make again the life-blood flow?"

As answering echo back on echo flies,
Reflected sorrow glistened in his eyes,
As he replied: "Daughter, I do. Make speed;
Bring hither in thy hand some mustard seed,
From the first home that thou canst find, where one
Hath never died, and I will heal thy son."

Back to the town, still bearing on her dead,
Koshagautami quickly, wildly sped,
And at the first low house her footsteps stayed,
And, with faint voice, her small petition made;
And as with trembling hand the seed she took,
Said with an eager and imploring look,
"Tell me, hath any in this home e'er died?"
Alas! the master bowed his head, and sighed,
"'Twas but last moon death seized my fairest one,
Him that my soul loved best—my first-born son!"

"The seed is worthless, then," she sadly said;
And to another dwelling quickly sped;

And on and on, until the day was spent.
But everywhere the sorrowing mother went,
She found a mightier one had been before,
And, with a sickened heart, she sought no more.

As alchemists, with patient, tireless thought,
Through centuries of time have vainly sought
Things not in Nature, yet have haply found
Their ill-directed efforts nobly crowned
With knowledge far more precious, far more great,
Than all their wildest fancies could create;—
So did this mother, in her fruitless task,
Find what she did not seek, and did not ask.
She found the seed that in each grief is sown;
Found that in sorrow she stood not alone;
And that the burden she accepted not
Was but the common fate, the common lot.
Ashamed that she had dared to murmur o'er
What all the world in silent suffering bore,
She took the child, and, in a lonely place,
Covered with moss and leaves his form and face,
Then came again where Buddha sat, and said,
"Master, I found no seed such as you bade
Me bring. There is no home without its dead."

" No, daughter; in this world of change and pain,
Thou long may'st ask and seek such seed in vain.
Thine eye hath seen, thy heart doth feel it true,
The dead are many, and the living few.
But hast thou in thy searching nothing found
That, like a ligature, thy grief hath bound?
The load beneath whose burden *one* would fall
Grows lighter if the weight is shared by *all*.
In shade and silence let thy grief be laid;
Earth has no home, no heart, without its dead."

A MOTHER'S REVENGE.

A MANIAC'S TALE.

LOOK on me, ye who idly pass this way;
 Aye, stop and gaze, as if, with horror filled,
Ye viewed a monster;—one from whose strong
    power
And frightful passions ye would shrink away.
Look well upon this bent-up, shrivelled form;
'Tis mightier than a giant's. See this hand,
Trembling and withered; it has strength with which
Ye dare not cope. But if ye'll stay and hear,
I'll tell of grief and suffering such as ye
Have never dreamed of; and when ye shall fall
Upon your knees to-night, pray God in heaven
That ye may never feel. Listen to me:
Fancy yourselves gifted, or cursed, by God,
As I have been, with passions deep and wild.
Stand ye where I have stood; bear what I bore;
Feel all that I have felt; suffer as I
Have suffered; turn each feeling to the light;

Probe to the quick each passion; and if ye
Can lift your hands to heaven, and say ye had
More patient been, and stronger to endure,
Then may ye pass harsh judgment upon me.

I once was young, and innocent, and gay;
Life was as dear, as beautiful, to me
As now it seems to you.   Each fleeting day
Brought new enjoyment; night, a calm repose.
Hope walked beside me, and the air was filled
With love's rich perfume.   To my lips,—
My eager, thirsting lips,—was pressed a cup
Full of delicious sweetness, and I drank.

I stood—a bride—beside the altar, as
A thousand forms, before and since, have stood.
With all the fervency of youth, I pledged
Myself to one, who gave his all to me.
If ye have known the freshness of young love;
If ye have had each longing passion stilled,
And every hour and every moment filled
With so much joy there was no more to crave,—
Then may ye feel what bliss was mine.
The newer longings of a newer life

God heard and answered; and I thought and said
That He was good.   A little form lay on
My breast; lips ravishing sweet met mine;
I looked in beauteous eyes whose depths disclosed
A new created world of rare delight.
My cup of joy, so brimming full before,
With rich and blissful happiness ran o'er.

        I thought my soul was more
Than filled with one; but when six children called
Me mother, there was room and love for all.
My first-born was my joy, my hope, my pride.
He was the fairest, dearest, best, where all
Were good and beautiful.   I had no thought
Apart from him; he filled my days with joy,
My slumbers with delight.   I could not tear
Him from my present or my future, and
The wonder was that I had ever lived
Without him.   Then the shadows fell across
My path; my boy began to fade and droop,
As doth a tender plant whose stalk is snapt.
A little hump between his shoulders grew,
At which my husband laughed, and said my fears
Were groundless, and as idle as a child's.

I sought the aid of science, and I watched
The doctor's face, as if within his hand
He held a fate more precious than my own.
His tones were cheerful, but his look was grave.
I knew my child was doomed. Words cannot paint
My agony of soul. I begged, as men
Beside the stake or scaffold have been heard
To beg for life, that he would save my boy.
He calmed me, saying that he had not thought
Of death; but—and he touched the little hump,
Then glanced across the street. My watchful eye
Followed him, as the fated victim doth
Its charmer, and I saw a hunchback pass,
Boys running at his heels, pointing at him,
With scoffs and jeers. "O God, be pitiful!
My boy,—my darling, beauteous boy,—my pride,—
To live, and be like that! Earth, open wide
A kindly grave, and hide him from my sight!"

So prayed my soul in its first agony.
Alas, for ignorance! I did not know
How suffering and affliction deepen love.
I did not know that every pain he bore
Would make him nearer, dearer to my heart.

I knew not that the fell, the bitter stroke,
Which severed him from others, would but bind
Him closer unto me.   The love I nourished
Deeper, wilder grew, until it was
No longer love, but soul-idolatry.

Months—years—passed by, and wrought a wondrous
    change.
Things somehow twisted and distorted grew;
Whether 'twas I or others, would be hard
For tongue to tell.   It may be I had grown
Unloving and unlovable;—God knows.
My husband had become indifferent
And cold to me;—harsh, cruel, to my child.
I little minded what he gave to me,
But when cross words, and heavy, stunning blows
Came to my boy, the creeping, sluggish blood
Leaped with a fever heat from vein to vein,
And passions, that before had calmly slept,
Coiled 'round the very centre of my soul,
Raged fierce and wild, and would not be subdued.
I saw my son grow fearful of his sire,
Shrink from his glance, and shudder at his step.
Oh! it is terrible when that dear name,

Which ought to be a sheltering tower of strength,
A fountain of delight, becomes a dread
And terror, and the place that ought to be
A miniature of heaven, an earthly hell,
Where every sinful passion is unchained,
And discord, hatred, dwell,—a place from which
We long to flee, but cannot get away.

My boy was never aught but beautiful
To me. His face was like a fair, fresh flower
Upon a rude, unsightly rock; or as
A limpid, placid lake, enclosed by rough
And rugged cliffs. His growing mind was like
A jewel set in stone; his deep, rich thoughts,
Clothed in the choicest drapery of words,
Revealed the mighty reservoir of wealth
Hid in that mis-shaped form. His eye was of
Heaven's deepest blue; his brow of purest snow,
On which the soft hair fell, like sunny beam;
His lip was pale, and beautifully carved ;
His smile was not the meteor's quick, bright flash,
'Twas lingeringly sweet, as sunset hues.
His voice was softer than a flute; no sound
In nature hath a depth so rich and full.

His hand was thin, and delicate, and white,
And its cool touch soft as a loving woman's.
Oh, if ye know aught beautiful and dear,
'Tis what my boy was like! If ye have one
Ye prize above all others,—one for whom
Ye would lie down and die, then is that one
Like my dear, sainted boy.

       One day the father came,
And said his child was growing like a girl;
That he must go and learn to be a man;
Must rough it with the world; must measure strength
With boys, and not for ever hang upon
A woman's hand.
I said he should not go. He said he should.
I told him there were five; that he could take,
Or one, or all, if he would only leave
This stricken one with me. But he said, "No."
I knelt. Upon my knees, to sinful man,
I prayed as unto God. I prayed and wept.
He only spurned and thrust me from his feet.
Then, after a long, bitter strife, after
Harsh, biting words, which, for slow, weary years,
Have eaten, like a canker, in my heart,

I yielded;—yielded, for his arm was strong.
The world, and law, and custom, all were on
His side, and only right on mine; and ye
Well know that they have power enough to crush
Both truth and right to dust.

They bore him to a school, long widely famed
For its harsh discipline, its meagre fare,
Its almost Draco laws.   'Twas leagues from home;
And when the boy wept sore and clung to me,
And said that he would die if sent away,
I marvel that I could have let him go;
But when his quick eye saw I suffered too,
He locked his feelings in his breast, and wept
No more; but mutely took his place within
The noble line of martyrs.   O my boy!
Could I but bring thee back;—could I but see
Thee as I saw thee then,—not earth and hell
Combined should take thee from me! I would hurl
Defiance at them all; and, seizing thee,
Would fly to some lone spot, and, if I could
Not live, would die with thee!

                My only pleasures were
The letters that he wrote, and mine to him.

My two great eras were the day he left,
And that he would return.

     One quiet noon,
After the whirl of morn had calmed away,
My husband came in hastily, and laid
A letter in my hand. A sudden fear
Seized on me, piercing to the very quick.
The paper quivered, rattled in my hand,
It trembled so. My sight grew dim, my brain
Confused; the letters were so indistinct,
And blurred, and running all together, that
I could not read. And then my husband spoke:
"Our boy is ill; and we will go to him."
It was as if he said, "Our boy is dead."
My palsied tongue kept silence, but I looked
At him, and if a glance has power to speak,
Then did mine say, "He's dead! and by your hand."

       We travelled side
By side, yet neither spoke a word. I know
Not what he thought; but as for me, I *knew*
My boy was dead. And when we reached the house
I looked to see the crape upon the knob;

And it was there.   They led us up broad steps
Into a little room where he had died.
The father stayed behind; he dared not look
On him he had so sorely, deeply wronged.

And I was glad.   I wished to be alone.
I found him stretched upon a narrow bed,
A single, tireless watcher at his side,
A pale-faced youth, who rose at my approach,
And left me with my dead.   I did not weep.
Grief such as mine knows not the shallow fount
Of tears.   I drew the white cloth from his face,
And looked,—looked full upon my idol, that
A mighty hand had in the night cast down.
His features were like chiselled marble in
Their calm and still repose.   His thin, pale hands,
Longer and whiter than before, were crossed
Above his breast.   No vestige of a smile
Lingered upon the wasted lips, that had
For ever closed with sighs of weariness.
The leaden-circled eyes half-opened were,
Yet dull and meaningless.   But oh, his brow,
His fair, white brow I had so often kissed,
Was just the same; and on it fell the soft

Bright hair, like cherub's golden wing.
I pressed his lips ;—they gave no kiss again.
I called him ;—but he heeded, answered not.
I lifted up the lids ;—the rayless orbs
So frightened me, I closed them from my sight,
And sank upon the floor ; yet did not weep,
Nor die. Death loves not to be wooed ; he flies
From those who seek him. 'Tis the happy die.
The wretched live.

A step behind aroused me, and I looked,
And saw the pale-faced boy, who came again.

        " What do you know
Of him ?" I asked ; " how grew he sick ? how died ?"

" He ne'er seemed well to me," he said, " and oft
I marvelled how his friends could send him here.
It takes an iron frame, a lion heart,
To scuffle with this cruel school-boy life.
But well I'll mind me what I say. These walls
Have ears—aye, tongues that can repeat.
But could I see his parents, I would tell
A tale that they would rather die than hear."

"Say on; I am his mother.   Never fear;
No harm shall come to thee.   Say all thou knowest."

" He died—well—just as many a sickly one
Has died before.   *They* say, grew sick and died:
I say, was starved and murdered.   Now this boy
Had tasks he *could* not learn, and then was starved.
How could he learn when he was faint for want
Of food and nourishment?   Lift up his form,
And see the marks of blows, and do not ask
Me how, or why he died?"

          "Hold, boy," I said,
" Will you stand here by death and God, and swear
That what you say is true?"   He laid one hand
Upon the corpse, raising the other, said,
"I swear."   "And I too swear," I cried; "swear by
This murdered boy,—by all the powers of heaven,
To be avenged!   Yet fear not thou, dear boy;
I would not harm one hair of thy young head."

          With tearless eyes
I saw my child laid in his narrow grave;
I saw them press and pile the cold, damp earth

Upon him, and I knew they wondering saw
My calmness; but I let them wonder. Then
When all was o'er, I said I wanted change—
Would see my sister, who lived far away.
I left; but went not near my sister's. I
Went to the place where he, my boy, had died;
I stole into the master's household; watched
Him there; noted his children one by one;
Saw how he smiled on this, and frowned on that.
I watched him in the quiet evening hours,
When life's sharp conflict, for a time, was o'er,
And all the thousand comforts he had brought
With his unrighteous gains were heaped around;
When art made warm the air and soft the light
Within the little world that he had formed.
And there, a living Nemesis, I stood,
Watching with flashing eyes and clenching teeth,
Hating with all my might, and brooding o'er
My wrongs, and nursing vengeance in my soul.
But what could he, poor man, what could he give
That would be half the value of the one
That I had lost?   But it was well for me
To take such as he had. This is earth's law
And justice, and 'twas mine. He killed by best

And dearest, and I claimed his most beloved.
I wanted life for life, and child for child!
And he loved best—not that young laughing girl,
Whose face was beauty's own, whose step was grace,
And tone was love's; nor yet the manly boy
Whose warm blood coursed with vigor through each
     vein,
Whose heart and form were strong with youth and
     health;—
But the sweet babe, whose cunning, winning ways
Made half the music of their happy home.
That one he loved; *that one* I marked my own.
Oh, how my spirit gloated o'er its prize!
How sweet was slow, long vengeance to my heart!
How did I draw the pictures of his own
And mine, until they were daguerreotyped
Upon my inmost soul. He had kind tones,
Sweet smiles, and soft caresses for his own;
Stern looks, harsh words, and cruel blows for mine!
The choicest food, the balmiest air, soft lights,
And silken couch for his:—hard, mouldy crusts,
Darkness, and cold, and heaps of straw for mine!

When none were near, I stole the little babe,

And bore him swiftly to my distant home,
And in the farthest cellar, damp, and cold,
And dark, I placed him.   Then I took revenge
And it was sweet.   I sat with forms
And voices all around, and when through floors,
And walls of stone, and oaken doors, I heard
The distant, muffled sound of infant's wail,
I laughed aloud, and triumphed in my joy!
Each day I went to see the little cheek
Grow thin and thinner, and with measured tape
Marked how the limbs were wasting day by day.
'Twas triumph's self to hear of searching wide,
And of the father's bitter agony,
Of great rewards, and armies of police.

Of all the men on earth I feared but one,
And he was of my household.   His keen glance
And searching gaze I could not bear to meet.
Methought he eyed me as the tiger eyes
His prey; and more than once I had resolved
To rid and free myself and earth of him.
Well, he, (my husband,) watched and followed me,
And found the child when it was almost dead,
And thwarted me, as he had always done,

And took the one sweet drop out of my life,
And brought, and keeps me here, because, forsooth,
I dared take vengeance in my hand!

They tell me years have passed since these things
        were.
I know not how to count and measure time;
The sunbeams struggling through the iron bars
Leave on these naked walls no numbering trace.
Tall, stately men and matrons visit me,
And say they are my children.   It may be.
But one absorbed my soul, and he is not;
The others are as naught.

There comes, at times, a white-haired, saintly man,
Who talks to me of God, and hope, and heaven.
I love to hear him, for his words are like
The dew upon the flinty rock, which, though
It does not soften, moistens it.   I say
He speaks of hope and heaven; and hope to me,
Is the blest thought of seeing my beloved,
And heaven is where he is.

Start not; you have your reason,—mine is gone.
Does your God seek what He hath borne away?
Or reason ask, when reason is withdrawn?
I wait,—the years are long,—I wait and pray
That He will send a little hand to clip
Life's worn out thread, and give me back my lost!

THE ORPHANS:

OR, "OUR FATHER IN HEAVEN."

IN a rickety house of a close, narrow street,
  Where suffering and sorrow were wont to re-
     treat,
Two pale little children sat watching the bed
Where their mother was sleeping, as wan as the dead.

'Twas a comfortless room, with its old broken panes,
And its dark, crumbling walls, that were covered
    with stains;
With only the bare, chilling floor for a seat,
And a pile of white ashes, long guiltless of heat;
With only the flickering, glimmering light
Of a candle, to make less hideous the night;
With a heap of damp straw for the sick woman's
    bed,
And nothing but hope for the near morrow's bread.
With a motion of suffering, the poor sleeper stirred,
The eyelids unclosed, but the lips gave no word.

Then a quick little watcher raised gently her head,
And the thin, tattered coverlet tried to respread;
And she smoothed the rough hair with a womanly
 stroke,
And full of kind love were the words that she spoke.

"You are better, dear mother; how sweetly you
 slept,
While brother and I have so quietly kept!
I thought 'twould be so when I drew on your cap;
There's no physic so good as a nice little nap."

"No, darling; my words you must try to believe;
You well know your dear mother would never de-
 ceive.
Think not I am better;—this calm is the breath,
And this freedom from pain is the numbness of death."

The little girl moaned;—"Oh, what do I hear?
Can we work, can we live, with our mother not near?
We never will trouble, we never will grieve;
O mother, sweet mother, for us try to live!
Oh, what will become of me when you are gone?
Me—friendless, and fatherless, motherless one?"

"Dear sister, can't God make our mother get well,
If He does the kind things I have oft heard you tell?"

"Yes, brother, He can; He does good, and not ill;
And I've asked Him so often I think that He will."

"Dear children, we know that with God is the power
To afflict, and to heal; to exalt, and to lower;
And we know that His wise, His unerring behest
Is not as we think, but as He knows is best.
If it pleases Him now your dear mother to take,
That mother well knows He will never forsake
The heart that to Him its all can confide,
And can own Him as Father, as Friend, and as Guide.
Whatever is taken, whatever is given,
Trust hopefully, children, your Father in heaven!"

Just then, with a sound of the mournfullest strain,
The rough wind swept in through the thin, broken
          pane,
And through the bare room he went searching around
With a whisk, and a whirl, and a furious bound,
Till the candle's faint glimmering caught his eye,
And he quickened his pace as he went whistling by,

Bearing on, like a victor, along his wild track,
The spark that, till then, held the deep darkness back.

With a shuddering awe the little ones crept
To their sick mother's side, and piteously wept;
But softly and fondly she silenced each moan,
With a tremulous touch, and an unmoved tone,
As she quietly bade them beside her lie,
And then folded her hands, in the darkness to die.

  In smiles the morn awoke;—awoke
   As if there were no pain;
  As if he never glad dreams broke
  Of those who, when they felt the stroke
  Of pitying slumber's welcome yoke,
   Hoped ne'er to wake again.
When Death, the iron king, held court,
It seemed almost a mocking sport
For the bright, smiling morn to come,
And flood with light that wretched room,
And wake to suffering and to tears
Children grown old with grief—not years.
And yet it came from the same Hand
That sped the darkness o'er the land;

The very same that soothes and grieves,—
That lowers and lifts,—that takes and gives.

The first one to waken to suffering and life
Was the youngest—the boy,—too young for such
　　strife.
There was nothing but hope in his wakening start,
There was nothing but trust in his innocent heart;
But not for the world would he utter a word
Till he saw that his sister from slumber had stirred.

"See, sister, she's sleeping; she's better, I know;
How I love just to look at her slumbering so!"

The little girl gazed, and then drew in her breath;
She had looked once before on the features of death;
But her voice trembled not, as softly she spake,
"She's not sleeping—but dead. She will never
　　awake."

"Oh, yes, she will waken; I'm certain she will."

"Nay; just touch her; you see she is cold—cold—
　　and chill."

"And so are we cold; and the room is all cold.
No wonder she's chilled in this dark, dismal hold.
Oh, I wish I had something to make a bright fire!
'T would warm her to watch it rise higher and
    higher."

"No, brother; it all would be worse than in vain;
She is gone, and we never can warm her again."

"Gone away!" said the boy, with a tear in his eye;
"Would she go, and not kiss us, and tell us 'Good-
    bye'?"

"The angels came down when the darkness was
    deep,
And they took her away while we both were asleep."

"And what shall *we* do?—we, so little and weak,
All alone in the world? What friend can we seek?"

"Not alone, dearest brother; we'll mind what she
    said
In the night, when her hands were placed on each
    head:

' Whatever is taken, whatever is given,
Trust hopefully, children, your Father in heaven.'
The morning has come; we will kneel at her side,
And will pray that He now for us both will provide.
You know we must *ask* what we wish to be given,
And there's no one to ask but the Father in heaven."

And then on the still morning air there arose
The words and the wish such a faith only knows.
They knew when they'd prayed, they had done all
      they could,
And, calm in that knowledge, they trustingly stood,
In quietness waiting beside the cold dead
For the Father in heaven to send them their bread!

Of the millions of prayers that winged their way
In the fresh, balmy air of the opening day,
Not one was there louder or mightier said
Than that of the orphans beside their dead.
It went through the room, and it went through the
      street,
Like the flash of the lightning, clear, vivid, and fleet;
It rose on the air, like a spirit forgiven,
Till it reached the bowed ear of the Father in heaven.

With magic stroke, it ripples woke,
   In the great sea of thought;
The swelling circles widened out,
   As if a heart they sought,
That suffering much, believing much,
Could beat responsive to their touch.

And such heart did they reach in a passer-by,
Who paused at the sound of the children's cry.
Through the broken glass he had seen them kneel,
And heard words that could soften a heart of steel;
But he reverently stood by the half-open door
Till the touching prayer of the children was o'er.
Then softly he entered. One look round the room
Told plainly the tale of their sorrow and gloom.
At sight of a stranger the little ones crept
To the pallet of straw, as though they still kept
Their confident trust, as ever of yore,
In the mother that never had failed them before.
But kindly he asked them the cause of their grief,
And gently and tenderly proffered relief.

To their mother they pointed, and sobbingly said,
"She was all that we had, and you see she is dead.

We did all we could that she easy might be,
But she died in the night, and we could not see.
We slept in the darkness, and she was alone
When she went to the place where death is un-
    known.
And there's none to take care of us, none to us
    given,
Unless it may be—the good Father in heaven!"

Oh! if it be anguish to die when the ones
That love us are near,—when the tenderest tones
And the kindliest of hands are smoothing the way,
While the cold touch of death is unfastening each
    stay,—
What must it be in the darkness to die,
When we know that no heart, no hand, can be nigh!

If it's hard for a mother her babes to confide
To the hand of another herself has long tried,
What must the faith of that parent have been
In the One she had trusted without having seen,
When alone she could leave helpless babes at her
    side.
So sure that the God she had served would provide!

If it's hard to give up even *one* that we love,

When the void is soon filled as the years onward move,

How strong must the hearts of those children have
      been

As they saw the last hand upon which they could
      lean

Grow lifeless and cold,—yet could turn from that
      dust

Above and beyond, with a Christian-like trust,

And, though from their reach every helper seemed
      driven,

Could so hopefully cling to their Father in heaven!

Oh, there was the fountain of tenderest love,

And there was the faith that mountains could move!

The good man wept sore as he drew to his side

The children who had none but God to provide,

And he asked, "Will you go to my bright, pleasant
      home,

Where suffering and want such as yours cannot
      come?"

But the little girl sighed, and shook sadly her head,

As she meaningly glanced at the form on the bed.

Then he spake once again: " When we 've laid her to
    rest,
And the earth has been placed above her still breast ?"

And she said, " We will go, and we ask not your name,
Nor whither you take us, for surely you came
From Him who provideth whatever is given,
And who careth for all—the good Father in heaven!"

OLD LETTERS.

I KEEP them still, though faded now and worn,
And of each trace of beauty long since shorn;
To strangers' eyes a tattered pile and old,
Fit to be stored in some neglected hold,
With all the rubbish that we cast away,
As if unworthy of the light of day.

And yet, from all that heaping round me lies
To charm with grace or use fastidious eyes,
Were I at danger's sudden call to wake,
And bid my heart its valued treasure take,
This faded packet with its yellow strings
Would find a place among her precious things.

From many a quiet, happy, peaceful home
These fleet-winged messengers of love have come;
O'er many a weary mile of land and sea,
Have safely brought their costly freight to me;
Brought to my sight, with more than human art,
The priceless coinage of some loving heart.

The skill of man has taught the sun to trace
And fix the lineaments of form and face;
Wrung from inexorable Time and Death
Part of their stolen prey—a shade—a breath;
But these can paint with higher, nobler art
The lasting photographs of mind and heart.

As when, by life's sharp conflicts roughly toss'd,
Before the portraits of the early lost,
We love, at times, in quietness to stand,
And look with yearning heart and outstretched
          hand;
So on these pictures of my happier days
I love, with soft and sad regret, to gaze.

They are not dead to me,—but fresh, and rife
With all the glow of animating life;
Not homely,—they are bright, and true, and fair;
Not worthless,—mines of richest wealth they bear;
Not dumb,—but ever eloquent with word,
And thought, and tone, affection loves to hoard.

They are to me no rude, unsightly heap,
But sacred tombs, where hallowed memories sleep;

Where, on the rest-days of a working life,
I love to turn from toil, and care, and strife,
And o'er these urns of hearts, and hopes, and years,
Let fall the sorrowing spirit's soothing tears.

Time holds enough, relentlessly and fast,
Within his wormy, mouldering, coffined past;
Enough within that cold, decaying grave,
I would have died a thousand times to save;
With my life's treasures, as in sport, he played,
Grasping the substance,—let me keep the shade!

Keep, as the blinded Eastern devotee
The sacred stone no Christian eye may see;
Keep, as the miser keeps his shining gold,
Safe in my house and spirit's strongest hold;
Keep, till the life-long sacrifice is made,
And heart and memory in one grave are laid!

FAMILY PORTRAITS.

I GAZE upon them, one by one,
　　Those faces loved so well of yore;
And weep to think that on this earth
　　Those faces shall be seen no more.

Oh! they were young, and fair and good,
　　And life was but a joy to them;
And they had strong, enduring hearts,
　　That floods of ill and wrong could stem.

They came,—they lingered for a while,—
　　They blessed the homes that gave them birth;
They hallowed every joy and grief,
　　Made dearer life, and fairer earth.

They vanished—as the hues of morn;
　　They died—as dies the summer breeze;
They swept like phantoms by, and left
　　Naught but a cold, white stone—and these:

These silent, changeless semblances,—
　　These beckoning shades that mock my sight;
These fleshless, bloodless forms, that cast
　　O'er memory's waste a meteor light,

And bring again long vanished joys,
　　That mingle strangely with earth's din;
And words and tones that, but for these,
　　I could believe had never been.

O eyes, that kindled at my sight!
　　O lips, once wont to smile on me!
O hands, that warmly clasped my own,
　　Your sameness is but mockery!

I mourn—and still ye calmly smile;
　　I weep—ye see unmoved the tear;
I stretch my pleading hands, I call;
　　Ye do not heed, ye will not hear.

I cannot gaze on features loved
　　As yours, and think ye thus estranged;
Ah no!—ye are to-day the same:—
　　'Tis only life and I have changed!

For ye do speak; your voiceless lips
　　And changeless smile have but one tone,
Which bids my fainting soul be strong
　　To do, and bear, and suffer on.

Then let me steal from earth away,
　　Steal from its pangs, its strifes, its storms;
And, like a pilgrim to his shrine,
　　Come oft, and gaze on your still forms,—

Until your calmness falls on me,
　　As evening shadows on the hill;
And I, upon life's changing tide,
　　Can look as ye, unmoved and still.

"I COUNT ONLY THE HOURS THAT ARE SERENE."

MOTTO ON A SUN-DIAL IN VENICE.

I LET the heavy days go by—
    The days of woe when pain is queen;
Let pass the sorrow and the grief,
    And "count the hours that are serene."

Quicker the creeping shadows glide
    If memory does not intervene;
Unsought they come, unnoticed die—
    "I count the hours that are serene."

I mark the sunbeam,—not the shade;
    Of brightness, not of darkness, glean;
I know not how to trace the clouds,—
    "I count the hours that are serene."

O passers on the road of life,
    O dials of a sun unseen,
Would ye of bliss the secret learn?
    "Count but the hours that are serene."

LIFE.

WHAT is it?—essence?—spirit?—breath?—or
    power?
That universal, fine, ethereal thing,
Stretched o'er a thousand years, or to an hour
    Compressed;—now coming and now vanishing?
Behold, within a world sustained by heaven,
    Where all with vexing mystery is rife,
The greatest, noblest boon to mortals given,
    The grandest mystery of nature—life.

The part that we may see, the part we know,
    Is but an atom of the mighty whole;
Is as one bud to all the flowers that grow,
    One blade to all the grass whose leaves unroll;
Is as a rushlight to the noon-day sun;
    One grain to all the sands of ocean's shore;
One stroke to all the toil conceived or done;
    One infant wail to grand Niagara's roar.

Beyond created time it stretches back,
    In thick, impenetrable folds entwined;
And sweeping on in deepening, widening track,
    Leaves thought and calculation far behind.
Conception strains its utmost power in vain
    To grasp the dark, mysterious One in Three;
And droops ere it can find the subtile chain
    That binds the was, and is, and is to be.

As shipwrecked mariner on drifting spar,
    Aroused to consciousness, as from a trance,
Darting his wild, despairing eyes afar,
    Beholds one boundless, fathomless expanse;
So we, still drifting, drifting on, may send
    Our longing gaze behind, before, and see
On neither side, beginning, course, nor end;
    Only a shoreless, vast immensity.

Life is the fiat of the Eternal One;
    An emanation of the Will Divine;
The breath of Him who speaks and it is done;
    The working of His deep and wise design.
His gift, incomprehensible and vast,—
    Magnificent and god-like:—and to be,—

To be, and last as He Himself shall last,
   Is our eternal and fixed destiny.

O thought sublime and terrible!—to be
   Part of the Centre that upholdeth all;
Part of the Infinite and only free,
   To rise eternal, or eternal fall!
For life is all in one grand largess given;
   It is to stand where holy angels fell:
It is a bliss ineffable in heaven,
   But deepest, direst misery in hell.

We may not choose:—who draws the breath of
     God,
   However feebly, draws that breath for ever.
Unconscious heirs, we change our state, our road,
   We change our world—we end existence never.
Life is the horologe whose secret springs
   Our rude, rough hands may never press upon;
'Tis the projectile the All Powerful flings
   In empty space that must move ever on.

Sooner might we exclude the light of day,
   Call on the flowers to bloom, or winds to blow;

Sooner might animate the senseless clay,
    Bid comets stand, or rivers cease to flow;
Might make of stars a pathway for our feet,
    Or laws to other, higher worlds decree;
Or hurl th' Eternal from His heavenly seat,
    Than for a single moment cease to be!

Strip life of its externals; lay it bare
    Of honor, wealth, and comfort; yet if free
From crime's polluting touch, it still is fair,—
    Aye more,—'tis great and glorious to be!
With lips of dust to draw the kingly breath
    Whose source and fountain is eternity;
And, sheathed in mail impregnable to death,
    As God, and angels, and just men,—to be!

O mortal, where and whatsoe'er thou art,
    Outcast and banned, this yet remains to thee;
Lift up thy drooping head, and let thine heart
    Rejoice in that thou art—rejoice to be!
O peer and mate of angels, even now
    A radiant light on thy lone path doth shine;
A crown of glory rests upon thy brow,—
    The boon of immortality is thine!

TO MY BOOKS.

COMRADES long tried!—friends of my lonely
    heart!
Who ne'er to me could aught but joy impart,
I love to gaze on your familiar forms—
The same through summer's suns and winter's storms,
And feel, whate'er I am, where'er I range,
There are *some* things that weary not, nor change.

I have been in the world, and I have sought
Its glittering scenes—its maddening pleasures bought.
With hot and thirsting lip, advanced to drain
Its proffered cup of mingled joy and pain:
And as the man who long at Bacchus' shrine
Hath knelt, turns sickened from the sparkling wine,

To purer streams that kindly nature gives,
And, like a child, stoops down, and drinks, and lives,

So does my weary, aching heart, grown tired
Of joys that sated not, though long desired,
Turn to the ever-gushing fount, where first
This eager spirit slaked its burning thirst.

Ye never turned from me in proud disdain,
Laughed at my ignorance, nor mocked my pain;
Ye never chid me for perception slow,
But patiently, with tender voice and low,
As doth a mother, ye went o'er and o'er
The lessons learned with labor long and sore.

No cold neglect your warmth could ever chill,
No wilful wanderings your chidings still;
How turns to-day my eager heart, with true
And yearning tenderness, again to you!
To you—that life's sharp pain the more endears!
To you—the tried and faithful friends of years!

Soothe me, as once of yore, with winsome art,
Ye soothed to rest my panting, feverish heart;
Raise from the dust this mute, despairing soul,
Show to these downcast eyes a loftier goal;

4

With mercy's hand your sparkling cordial give,
That these faint lips may drink once more, and live!

In my still chamber wide unfold to me,
Scenes that mine eyes have vainly longed to see;
Tell me of all the great and good of earth,
Of suffering patience, and of struggling worth:
Rehearse each noble thought, each glorious deed,
Till spirit shall on kindred spirit feed.

With power prophetic, and magician art,
Sound to its lowest depths the human heart;
Bring to the light the hidden things of time,
The hoarded, prized, and sought of every clime:
Wage with decay and change a ceaseless strife,
And give the dead the form, the voice of life.

Teach me to emulate their noble deeds,
To turn my feet where stainless glory leads;
Climbing like them the rugged road and rough,
Following their footsteps, though it be far off;
And, like Elisha, gaze, until on me
May fall the *shadow* of their drapery.

Like them, the good, the lofty, and the true
Of life, with constant, tireless heart pursue;
Like them, a faithful, friendly light hold forth,
Over the wild, dark paths and moors of earth;
Breathing the words that point men on and higher,
Touched, like the prophet's lips, with holy fire!

A SIMILE.

THE restless water strives
  And struggles in its course;
Its single, constant aim to reach
  The level of its source.

And so the fettered soul,
  Through mist, and film, and clod,
Is ever striving to attain,
  Its source and fountain—God.

TO AN INFANT.

LITTLE stranger, dost thou come
    Seeking on this earth a home?
Nestler in thy mother's heart,
Dost thou seek with us a part?
Seek the pleasure and the woe
Mingled in each cup below?

Joy of earth, and heir of heaven,
Child of love, in mercy given;
Drawing us with winning ways
Back to our own infant days:
Blessed days! when we within
Were as free as thou from sin;

When we fondly look as now
On thy fair, thy stainless brow;
And with hearts that know so well,—
As our own worn spirits tell—

What the strife of earth must be;
Can we gladly welcome thee?

Welcome thee with joy among
Life's soul-weary, laboring throng?
Welcome thee to pains and tears,
Mocking hopes and sorrowing years?
Welcome thee, sweet, guiltless one,
To each grief that we have known?

Yes! with hearts that know full well
What the lips refuse to tell;
Know the bitter pangs and strife;
Know the joys, the bliss of life;
And its depths, its fulness see
Gladly do we welcome thee.

For thou hast the power to bless
In our hours of bitterness;
And with winsome smile and voice
Thou dost bid us here rejoice;
Pointing, as we onward glide,
To the brightest, sunniest side.

And we know life endeth not
With earth's weary, sorrowing lot;
But above, beyond the sky,
Is thy spirit's destiny;
And we watch thee fitting here
For thy higher, holier sphere.

SUMMER EVENING.

A DOWN the West,
In crimson dress'd,
The kingly sun sinks to his rest;
And robed in state
Meet for the great,
The clouds, like princely courtiers, wait.

The weary Day
Sees pass away
To feebler hands his powerful sway;
And from his seat,
With blushes sweet,
'Bends low his sister, Night, to greet.

In distant view,
The mountains blue
Blend with the skies their changeless hue,
As if they strove
In deed to prove
Our nearness to the world above.

The gushing note
From birdling throat
Across the fields hath ceased to float;
But 'round the hill
The tricksome rill
In measured cadence ripples still.

With transient blaze,
The fire-fly strays
O'er many a wild and tangled maze;
And loud and shrill
The whip-poor will
Repeats his sad, unvaried trill.

Then all about,
As half in doubt,
The trembling stars peep coyly out;
And like a pall,
Enrobing all,
The deepened shades and shadows fall.

FROM A WIFE, TO HER HUSBAND.

IF I have sought by art the gifts
    Of nature to supply,
Or ever asked for beauty's charm,
    'Twas but to please thine eye.

If I with labor strove to make
    The stores of learning mine,
'Twas that I might befittingly
    As thy companion shine.

If I have ever seemed to seek,
    With tireless zeal, for fame,
'Twas that thy heart with pride might thrill
    At mention of my name.

The praise of other lips than thine
    Is less than naught to me;
I know no world where thou art not,
    No life apart from thee!

THE BLUE RIDGE.

O MOUNTAI 'S of Blue, like sentinels guarding
    The vale and the plain with vigilance true,
Like bulwarks of strength, or citadels warding,
    Unyielding ye stand, sweet Mountains of Blue.

Ye rise like monarchs of proud, olden spirit,
    Receiving the homage they feel is their due;
Like genius, exalted by virtue and merit,
    Far off and above us, sweet Mountains of Blue.

Like Faith, holy Faith, who, serene and undaunted,
    Still bears on her forehead heaven's pure, beaming
        hue;
And walking a world by sin and guilt haunted,
    Yet points us above, sweet Mountains of Blue.

Ye catch the first glimpse of the smile-beaming morn-
    ing,
  Whose clear, heavenly rays your glories renew;
And with sunlight and purple your summits adorning,
  In splendor they crown you, sweet Mountains of
    Blue.

When day has departed, and evening has lighted,
  With soft, quiet beauty, each tranquilling view,
The splendors of morn, noon, and eve, are united
  In glory around you, sweet Mountains of Blue.

Time sweeps from our grasp the hopes that we cherish,
  Change marketh the paths our footsteps pursue;
Yet ye stand while men rise, flourish, and perish,
  For ever the same, sweet Mountains of Blue.

Fair emblems of truth, unchanged and unchanging,
  Though tempests may veil awhile from our view;
Beyond the dark clouds and thunderbolts ranging,
  Like truth above error, sweet Mountains of Blue.

No wonder the heathen bow down and adore you,
  So majestic, and grand, and unchangeably true;

Had I stood like them, untutored, before you,
    I too would have worshipped, sweet Mountains of
        Blue.

And now, when away from time's bitter strife turning,
    I seek the pure joys of my youth to renew,
I gaze on your summits, and with you returning,
    Greet high, holy visions, sweet Mountains of Blue.

For if ever the peace heaven giveth here fills me,
    If ever the world recedes from my view,
It is when the light of a Sabbath-eve thrills me,
    Beneath your pure azure, sweet Mountains of Blue.

Let me stand, though earth's tempest's around me are
        driven,
    Serene, and unmoved, and unyielding, like you;
With my heart and my eyes still lifted to heaven,
    For ever the same, sweet Mountains of Blue.

Bend o'er me while life's pulses through me are leap-
        ing,
    Speak to me of thoughts and deeds, noble and true;
And when low in silence and dust I am sleeping,
    Keep watch o'er my ashes, sweet Mountains of Blue.

WHAT IS LIFE'S GREATEST BLESSING?

I ASKED the sick man, and he said, " 'Tis health."
I asked the poor man, and he answered, " Wealth."
I asked the lonely prisoner. " Ah!" said he,
" The greatest boon of life is to be free."
I asked the laborer, with toil oppressed.
He wiped his aching brow, and answered, " Rest."
So I have learned this truth,—that each man counts
Life's greatest blessing is the one he wants.

SYMPATHY.

After all, it is but a little way that our friends can go with us, and sympathy, like every .hing human, has bounds that it cannot pass.

I HAVE had friends—and they were dear;
    How dear, this heart, so fondly keeping
Sad vigils o'er them year by year,
    Tells in its secret, ceaseless weeping.

I have had friends—and they were true
    To every pulse of generous feeling;
Their memory o'er me, like the dew,
    With fragrant freshness now is stealing.

But in my bosom hangs a veil
    Before the holiest of her holies;
No common priest the covering frail
    May lift to scan its depths or glories.

For feelings lie beyond the reach,
    The softest, tenderest touch of mortal,
That cannot don the robe of speech,
    Nor pass the spirit's outer portal.

A little way along life's path
　　Friends come, not leading, following rather;
For unto them the Master saith,
　　"Thus far ye may go, and no farther."

Thus far,—it is the clasp of hand,
　　The tone that says, "I also suffer;
My feet have pressed as cold a strand,
　　And trod a pathway lonelier, rougher."

And this is all.　Up the steep sides
　　We climb, there is for them no wending;
And down into the flowing tides
　　And hidden depths there's no descending.

Who leans his strength upon the reed,
　　The broken reed of human feeling,
Will find within his sorest need
　　A wound that hath no balm of healing.

The soul that finds on earth no rest,
　　No heart to share its choicest treasure,
Must seek that higher, stronger breast
　　Whose heights and depths *she* cannot measure.

TO MY SEWING NEEDLE.

I NEVER loved thee.   In my earlier days
  I scorned and shunned thee.   To my childish gaze
Thy skilful nimbleness and shining form
No beauty brought, no potency or charm;
I only viewed thee, spurning all thy pleas,
Sworn foe to freedom, idleness, and ease.

But thou hast clung to me in spite of all,
Like a true friend, who minds not change or fall;
I have not found—existence never gave—
More ready, willing, and obedient slave;
And somehow I have come to look at thee,
If not with pleasure, with complacency.

It may be as the galley-slave has learned
Something of love for toil that once he spurned;
Or as a man, condemned for life to dwell
A prisoner, grows in time to like his cell.
Many the things 'tis wise to take in gross—
Few feelings can be analyzed too close.

TO MY SEWING NEEDLE.

I ought to love thee.   Thou hast ever been
To sorrowing woman near as blood in kin;
And many an hour of anguish hast thou whiled,
As back and forward thou hast flashed and smiled,
Bringing sweet memories and pleasant thought,
As fair and graceful figures thou hast wrought.

Thou hast from Nature borrowed light and shade,
Hast many an ancient battle-scene portrayed;
Wrought banners men were proud to wave on high,
Decked castle walls with gorgeous tapestry;
The transient, perishing of earth engraved,
And noble deeds and words of wisdom saved.

Thou hast filled homes with plenty; thousands wait
On thee, as mendicants at castle gate;
Thou hast the naked clothed, the hungry fed,
Adorned the blushing bride, and robed the dead;
And worlds of might work by thine unseen aid,
Since thou by Dorcas hast been sacred made.

O power so small and silent, yet so strong,
And wonder-working of the laboring throng,
Still be thy might, thy glory, felt and known,
And, in the van of life, still hold thy own;

TO MY SEWING NEEDLE.

Still keep thine ancient place at home and hearth,
Among the least, yet mightiest of the earth.

For long as thou dost there in honor reign,
The world may place her glittering baits in vain;
As long as thou dost in thy patience toil,
A might remains the tempter's power to spoil;
As long as thou dost help her to endure,
No charm can woman from her place allure.

LIFE'S LESSONS.

SPREAD o'er a page our sorrowing tears have
      blurred,
  Whose letters we know not by sight or sound,
  Whose syllables, so oddly, strangely bound,
Make up an unintelligible word
We vainly strive in memory to hoard,
  And whose design and beauty, use and end,
(Of which, as foreign things, we may have heard),
  Our childish spirits fail to comprehend.
Sometimes unwittingly, as breathed upon
  By inspiration, we may rightly call
A single letter, or, with sigh and moan,
  Upon a proper word may chance to fall;
But ere one half the meaning has been learned,
A newer and a harder page is turned.

THE PRESENT.

WHY need we to the dim, dark Past recede,
    And search her record for soul stirring deed,
When so much in the teeming Present lies
To animate our hearts, and fill our eyes?

Why need we seek to taint and soil our page
With horrors that disgraced a former age;
Or drag again, as curious things, to light
The sins it were more wise to hide from sight,—

When Time reveals no hour, and earth no place,
Where Crime shows not her bold, unblushing face;
And our sad Present bears enough,—enough
To crowd the page of warning and reproof?

Why search the darkness of a vanished night,
Or trace the glimmers of a dawning light,
When o'er our clearer path and higher way
Shines the full radiance of perfected day?

Why need we bid the quiet, sleeping dead
Again for us their bloody paths re-tread,
When bolder heroes through as loud a din,
Still walk the earth, still nobly strive and win?

No fires are kindled now, no stakes are driven,
To horrify the earth and insult heaven;
But still, unseen, the life-drops trickle down,
And suffering earns to-day a martyr's crown!

Earth's future heroes, glorious and wise,
Are given to our unconscious hearts and eyes;
And heaven's blest angels, through the shades and
      glooms,
Walk by our sides, and dwell within our homes.

We strive to grope into the shadowed Past,
Or o'er the Future our dim light to cast,
And let the present, freighted full, slip by,
Without one throb of heart, one glance of eye.

Time dulls the sinking echoes of the Past,
While o'er the Future Mercy's veil is cast;
And our short sight of life can see no more
Than a few steps behind, a few before.

Oh, could we view our lives, our days aright,
How would our hearts enkindle at the sight!
How would we droop, or lift our beaming eyes,
To see how low we fall, how high *might* rise!

THE GIFTS OF LOVE.

SHE gave not much, as counts the world,
    A little here and there;
A few small coins, a crust of bread,
    A softly whispered prayer.

She gave a kindly smile, a word
    Of comfort and of cheer;
A silent, loving clasp of hand,
    A sympathizing tear.

Blessed like the widow's mites, those coins
    Unclosed wealth's grasping hand;
Opened a gushing fount that spread
    Wide o'er the thirsty land.

That kindly smile, that cheering word,
    Fell on a breaking heart;
And closed and bound a wound unseen,
    And healed a secret smart.

That gentle, loving clasp which said,
   "Look up, O sister mine,"
Drew from the clutch of death a soul
   That shall in glory shine.

That whispered prayer, unheard on earth,
   So faintly was it given,
Rose on the spirit-wings of faith,
   And moved the throne of heaven.

Such were her gifts;—and half their worth
   By words can ne'er be told;
Nor is earth wise enough to heed,
   Or large enough to hold.

IN MEMORIAM.

FAREWELL!—I will not weep that thou
 Art resting with the blessèd now;
Or that the Father's wise design
Hath made thy path more short than mine.

Farewell!—a stronger than our love
Hath borne thee to thy home above;
And though the world may be less fair,
Heaven is more dear since thou art there!

MY DEAD.

I COUNT not those among my dead
  (Though from my sight and presence fled)
Whom, safe beyond the realms of change,
No time, no mortal, can estrange;
Their love and trust but brighter shine
Whom death has made for ever mine.

They are my dead who, living yet,
Make life one long and sad regret;
Who, false to every memory,
Still walk the earth, more dead to me
Than if, with chilling, threatening mien,
The cold, damp grave were walled between.

They are my dead—the vanished years
I mourn with unavailing tears;
The long-fled joyous years that seem
Like pleasant tale, or beauteous dream;
The full-pressed, teeming years that hold
Treasures ungathered and untold.

They are my dead—the hopes that sprung
In life's glad morning strong and young;
Yet nurtured with the tenderest care,
They faded like earth's bright and fair;
Perished, as sink into the grave
Whom neither love nor skill can save.

Uncovered to the gazer's eye,
Behold my dead unburied lie;
Like men, unshriven and unbless'd,
They cannot sleep in peaceful rest,
But loud above life's whirl and din,
They mock me with, " It might have been."

O Time, these dead, so cold and white,
Help me to bury from my sight;
Bury the mocking hopes and years,
Bury in silence, and in tears;
Bury them deep—they were too bright;
Bury them deep—far out of sight!

WHAT SHE COULD.

"She hath done what she could."

I CANNOT seek my Father's house,
  And in His temple pray ;
But in this quiet room my heart
  May silent homage pay.

I cannot toil as others do
  Along the world's broad mart ;
But where He placed me I can stand,
  With patient, watchful heart.

I cannot open wide my hand
  Whene'er the suffering plead ;
But I can bear their woes to Him
  Who doth the sparrows feed.

And when the whole is measured by
  Not what I *did*, but *would*,
It may be He will say of me,
  "She hath done what she could."

UNBELIEF.

'TIS strange when God throws wide His door
　　And lets the needy suppliant in,
Declaring he who asks shall have,
　　And he who strives shall surely win,
We do not oftener seek that door,
And freely ask and plead for more.

And strange that, after we have prayed,
　　And after God has heard our prayer,
And angels to our waiting hearts
　　The Father's ready message bear,
We marvel He should answer make,
And scarcely will the blessing take.

O fools, and slow of heart to trust
　　And feel His tenderness and power!
O fools, and slow to rest upon
　　The strength that is a mighty tower!
Afraid the promise to believe,
Afraid the blessing to receive!

SPERO, CREDO, FIDO.

I CANNOT tell man's labored proofs
    In subtile, rare device,
Of the Unseen, Eternal One,
    The Soul of mysteries.
The creature the Creator shows:
    I am—therefore He is.

I know not how Jehovah could
    With men in converse be;
Nor ask of that recorded word
    A learnèd proof to see:
I am too glad to think that God
    Has given a book to me.

I cannot tell how mercy may
    Justice and law survive;
Nor comprehend how Jesus' death
    Eternal life can give:

I only know that He hath said,
   "Look unto Me and live."

I know not how a dying breath,
   A human, sin-stained plea,
Can span the space 'twixt man and God,
   And alter heaven's decree;
But I have heard the Father's word,
   "In trouble call on Me."

I know not how life's ceaseless ills
   Can blessings antedate;
Nor how the bitter will be sweet,
   And crooked places straight;
'Tis written, "All will work for good
   To those who love and wait."

I cannot tell where heaven may be,
   Nor what its glories are;
Save that it waits the faithful soul,
   And God and Christ are there;
And that the happy spirits rest
   From sin, and death, and care.

For secret things belong to God,
    And not to finite dust;
And high as human mind may soar,
    It owns the wisdom just
That veils the deepest, and to man
    Gives hope, belief, and trust.

VOICE OF THE DYING.

WEEP not for me!
  I am the captive sighing
One glimpse of warm, reviving life to see;
  And this cold, hideous thing that ye call dying,
Is but the welcome friend that sets me free.

Weep not for me!
  I am the traveller weary,
Who o'er rough seas and deserts wild has come;
  And dreaming yet of pathways long and dreary,
With transport sees the gleaming lights of home.

Weep not for me!
  I am the sick one longing
For one brief respite from pain's ceaseless strife;
  Who in one moment through the visions thronging,
Sees in her grasp eternal health and life.

Rejoice for me!
My path was rough and dreary;
Faint was my heart, and torn my aching feet;
Life's burden pressed me sore, and I was weary;
The rest our Father gives is long and sweet.

Rejoice for me!
Even now do I behold Him
Whom I have loved, whom I have sought so long;
Even now my eager, spirit-arms enfold Him,
And these dull ears have caught the angel song.

Rejoice for me!
When ceased the labored watching,
Ye fold the hands above my painless breast;
And nevermore the low, faint whisper catching,
Ye close the weary eyes in endless rest.

Rejoice for me!
When o'er the hillock bending,
Where toil is not, and peace and stillness dwell,
And holy thought is ever heavenward wending,
Ye say with quiet heart, "She sleepeth well."

THE CAPTIVE.

WITHIN his grated cell,
 A captive sat and sighed;
His skeleton hand, like a shadow, fell
 On the tasteless crust at his side.
His hair was damp with the prison mould,
 His eye was hollow and wild;
And the arm that once could giants fell
 Was weaker than a child.

He, in that cell, for years
 Had waited, watched, and prayed,
Till, numb alike to hopes and fears,
 He asked and wished no aid.
A breathing corpse within a tomb
 No eye but heaven's could see;
All that he heard was his keeper's step,
 And the turn of the iron key.

Yet was there something that bound
 His senses still to earth;

To the world of action, light and sound,
    Of happiness and mirth.
A tiny sunbeam daily came
    From its home of joy and bliss;
And stole, as a living thing, to his side,
    And fell on his cheek like a kiss.

He watched and watched it fall
    Down through the rusty grate;
He saw it climbing o'er the wall,
    And o'er his fettered feet.
It sweetly spoke of bright green fields,
    Of trees, and cool, clear stream;
It said there was light and hope on earth,—
    Aye, light and hope for him.

Was he forgotten? No;
    Fond eyes had long been dim;
True hearts had shared his every throe,
    And lips had prayed for him.
But Evil can rule with iron hand,
    And Hatred is bitter and strong;
And what is the might of a woman's love
    Against the power of Wrong?

The captive raised his eye
　　To greet his sunny friend,
And breathed for it the latest sigh
　　His weary soul might send.
It came at last; and his eye grew bright
　　Watching its noiseless tread;
But when it reached the pallid cheek,
　　It lighted the face of the dead!

　　*　　　*　　　*　　　*　　　*

Weep not for him who lieth
　　On fields where fame is won;
But weep for him who dieth
　　A thousand deaths in one.
Aye, weep for him that languisheth
　　Where hope may never come;
Who, drop by drop, gives up his life
　　For liberty and home.

UNRECOMPENSED.

While Hope remained, I lived, I toiled ;—
Hope fled, life was of all despoiled
That gave it worth.

I DID not weep when Vandal hands
   My treasures bore away;
Nor when I saw the lurid flames
   My home in ashes lay;
But on the ruin gazed, and said,
   "O native Land, for thee
Far more than this I'd gladly bear,
   If thou may'st yet be free."

I did not weep when sorrowing men,
   With slow and measured tread,
Brought back the strong man of my house,
   To lay him with his dead;
But stilled the throbbing of my heart,
   And stifled down the sigh,
And said, "Tis great and glorious
   For one's own land to die."

And when the bitter ending came,
　　And all was given and lost,
And I was like a severed leaf
　　By wind and tempest toss'd,
I gathered up my strength, and said,
　　"The future yet remains,
And in her opening hands are laid
　　Strong, honest Labor's gains."

But, when I felt the bitterness
　　Of unrequited toil,
And saw the base and wicked rise,
　　Rich with the orphan's spoil;
When starving children cried for bread,
　　And there was none to give,
And all the weak were trampled down,
　　Just that the strong might live:

When every coming year disclosed
　　More labor and less gain,
And life was but another name
　　For weariness and pain;

When love at death bequeathed to love
  Such heritage of woe,
The tears that Hope so long had stayed
  Despair allowed to flow!

ANIMUS VIVIT.

WHAT though they level down each grave,
    Each character defame?
Blot from recording History's page
    Each grand, heroic name?
Honor shall bear aloft their palm,
And Song shall every deed embalm.

What though from every Southern field
    They raze each hallowed stone?
And scatter to the raging storms
    Each bleaching rebel bone?
Memory will still her treasures keep,
And Love will find a place to weep.

For men may bend the lightning's course,
    And check the flowing wave;
May teach the winds to do their will,
    The subtile light enslave;
But feeling was not made to be
The passive tool of tyranny.

Wherever base Oppression ruled,
　　Or outraged Freedom cried;
Or helpless innocence was wronged,
　　Is where they would have died.
And there will we, lamenting, stand,
With weeping voice, and lifted hand.

We *need* no sculptured stone to keep
　　The name of son and sire;
Our hearts shall bear their epitaphs
　　In characters of fire;
And Memory will be the grave
That holds the relics of the brave!

THE SOUTHERN CONFEDERACY.

LIKE a lioness roused by the tramping of foe,
　Like the pent waters bursting in wild, sudden
glow;
Like a city grown up in the darkness of night,
Like a star in full glory, it rose on our sight.

Like the path of a vessel swift cleaving the seas,
Like the love of the birds that is told to the breeze;
Like the glittering ice-jewels on sun-lighted spray,
Like youth's visions of beauty, it vanished away.

'Twas resistance aroused by the shriek of alarms;
It was courage defying the terror of arms;
It was manhood defending the altar and hearth;
It was liberty seeking a home upon earth.

It had fervor and zeal,—it had daring and youth;
It had justice, and reason, and honor, and truth;
It had battles and sieges, and glory's red wreath,
It had waiting, and watching, starvation, and death.

And its fall was the terrible crushing of right,
The triumph of envy, and hatred, and might;
The folding of hands that could struggle no more,
The spread wings of freedom forsaking our shore.

Let it rest in the slumber no horror can break;
Let it rest with the heroes who died for its sake;
With the grandeur no failure, no foe can o'ercast,
Let it rest in the hallowing tomb of the past.

As over the hill-tops, the valleys, and plains,
Though the sun hath departed, a glory remains,
So over its ruin and wreck may be seen
A splendor that shows to the world what has been.

As the pierced spirit calls for some moments to shed
In secret its drops o'er the loved and the dead,
Even thus do we give unto what was so dear,
One day for a thought,—for a sigh,—and a tear.

We might think it a dream,—but for hearts that are
    broken,
For high places still vacant,—for yon marble token;

We might think it ne'er was—but for freemen now
    slaves,
For homes laid in ashes,—for wounds,—and for
    graves.

For we *gave* not our own—it was wrested away;—
We bartered no rights—and we glory to-day
That we stood by the land that we could not deliver,
And our swords drank life-blood ere they laid down
    for ever!

THE SOUTH.

WE loved her when she sat queen among nations,
    A crown of glory on her radiant brow;
Rich with the incense of world-adulations,
    And strong in powers that right and truth endow.

When o'er her blooming plains and shining waters
    Plenty and Wealth swept on with even tide;
When noble-hearted sons and beauteous daughters
    Made glad her thousand homes of joy and pride:

When the Past gave no echoing sound of sorrow,
    The happy Present banished care away;
And the wished Future was the glad To-morrow,
    That lengthened and intensified To-day.

But more, far more, when with just indignation,
    At but the thought of cherished rights o'erthrown,
She rose against a vaunting usurpation,
    And dared assert, and dared to claim, her own:

When to the holy God of heaven appealing,
  She bared her breast to meet a murdering sword,
And with life-blood her words and actions sealing,
  Lost all she prized and sought, gained all she feared.

Yet more we love her as in desolation
  She mourns her name, her rights, her children gone,
And breathes but one wild wail of lamentation,
  Whose depth of agony might move a stone.

As the fond mother, who, when health is flowing
  In red, rich streams, but little heeds her child,
Finds warmer love and stronger feeling glowing,
  If suffering blight where late enjoyment smiled,—

So with hearts throbbing with a tenderer yearning,
  We gaze upon our prostrate, stricken land;
And with a deeper, wilder passion burning,
  Sad, tireless watchers at her side we stand.

Dearer her quivering form all scarr'd and gory,
  And faint with strife against a world of foes;
Dearer a thousand times her touching story
  Of unexampled sufferings, deeds, and woes.

And we are learning, like the hope-forsaken,
    To speak of her, our loved, our prized, our own,
Softly, as names of those whom death has taken,
    Are only breathed with low and reverent tone.

MISSION OF SONG.

EARTH was not banned to angels; myriad forms
    Speed here and there, on heavenly mission
       sent.
Earth was not cursed for them; its scathing storms
    Break not the even calm of their content.
Tireless and swift on wings of wind they go,
Nor other will than His who sent them know.

A thousand forms are 'round us;—noiseless feet
    Keep measured pace with ours o'er thorny wastes;
Eyes that we see not our dim glances meet,
    And strength, unsought, to our assistance hastes;
Hands that we feel not our worn fingers take,
And voices speak as never mortal spake.

One hath long walked with us; was with the stars
    That sang together when creation woke;
And close to man, through all life's shocks and jars,
    Hath made more strong his heart, more light his
       yoke.

We know not, ask not, if she may belong
To earth or heaven; but we have called her Song.

She hath a holy mission; it is hers
    To speed o'er every land, and clime, and race,
And rescue from oblivion, change, and years,
    The noble and sublime of every age and place.
When marble falls, and crumbles into dust,
Song, living Song, shall guard with care her trust.

She loves to dwell with Nature; she hath lent
    Her voice to wind, and bird, and stream, and sea;
There is no spot o'er which she hath not bent,
    No space she hath not filled with melody;
To listening ear there is no sound but brings
Some echo from her harp of thousand strings.

Through her Passion finds words, Love whispers soft,
    Anger and Hatred rage, and Sorrow weeps;
Through her Devotion quickens, soars aloft,
    Hope brighter smiles, and Faith more steadfast
        keeps.
Spirit communes with spirit, and hearts speak,
That else, all other voice denied, would break.

Lands have no history that have no song;
　　Their heroes lie forgotten in their graves;
No living voice awakens in their young
　　The emulating zeal that dares and braves:
The thought ungarnered and the deed unsung
Are treasures to the winds and waters flung.

She is the baffler of decay and time,
　　The wielder of a weapon keen and strong;
The bold discloser of high-seated crime;
　　The dreaded foe of tyrants and of wrong:
Oppression's power all right may crush—deny;—
But truth embalmed by Song can never die.

Well should *we* love thee; we, the tempest-toss'd,
　　Bereft of name and country; we, who cast
Our all on one wild, fearful throw, and lost
　　All but the waning memory of the past:
We give thee, noble and high-minded Song,
Our name, our deeds, our suffering, and our wrong.

Guard thou our unmarked dead; watch o'er their dust,
　　Embalm their actions, and their honor keep;

Tell how they fought and died with undimmed trust
   In God and Right, and with th' unconquered sleep;
Thy sweetest, softest, saddest notes belong
To her who has no history but—Song.

OUR FALLEN BRAVE.

[FOR MEMORIAL DAY.]

THEY lie 'neath many a marble shaft,
    Our noble, fallen brave;
They lie on many a battle-field,
    In many an unmarked grave.
They lie, by Honor guarded safe,
    In peaceful, dreamless rest;
They lie by every valiant heart
    And patriot spirit bless'd.

They come on this Memorial Day,
    They haunt the very air,
With scenes long passed, with forms long stilled,
    With words and deeds that were.
They come to mourning household bands,
    They come in heart and thought;

They come in struggles they have made,
  In battles they have fought;

They come,—and living voices speak
  Their names and deeds once more;
We give a flower,—a sigh,—and then
  Memorial Day is o'er.

O children dear, who never saw
  The old Confederate gray;
Who never saw our soldiers march
  With flag and drum away;
Who never saw the dead brought back,
  The wounded line the street;
Who never heard the cannon's roar,
  Nor tramp of victor feet;
Keep as a holy trust this day
  To their remembrance true,
Who, sorely tried, were faithful found,
  And fought and bled for you!

That so, though dead, they still shall live,
  Live on, as year by year,

This day recalls the memories
   So sacred and so dear.
Live on though ages o'er them roll;
   Live on in flower-wreathed grave;
Live on in hearts that cherish still
   Our own, our fallen brave!

THE NEW SOUTH.

SHE hath lifted her head, she hath loosened her
  bands,
She hath cast away ease from her life and her hands;
She hath put on her strength, like a robe, and come
  forth,
She will take her own place with the nations of earth.

Though her body hath laid as the ground and the
  street,
And the crown of her pride hath been trodden by
  feet,
She will rise, she will shine from a loftier height,
With a crown of new glory, a star of new light.

She hath wealth in her waters, and wealth in her
  lands,
And her fate and her destiny lie in her hands;
She hath muscle to labor, and skill to secure,
She hath boldness to venture, and strength to endure.

As the mother forgets not her child that is dead,
Though his grave is unknown, and his name is not
    said,
So her lost she remembers,—aye, clasps them to-day,
And deep in her bosom she hides them away.

She hath buried her past in the silence of years,
She hath turned her for ever from mourning and
    tears;
She hath shouldered the burden no love can make
    light,
And hath brought to the conflict her daring and
    might.

Will she win?—Just as sure as the storm-beaten tree
Rises firmer, and stronger, and grander, will she;
Just as sure as she holds with a grip hard and tight,
As her fathers before her, truth, honor, and right.

Her foes may malign her, may laugh at, and sneer,
But through all, like a ship o'er the waves, will she
    steer;
And the breath of detraction shall over her pass,
As harmless as shadow of cloud o'er the grass.

As the string that is stretched gives more clearly its
    sound,
As in flowers that are crushed sweetest perfume is
    found;
As after the tempest come sunshine and calm,
And after the battle the laurel and palm,—

So clearer, and sweeter, and brighter will she
Shine out of her gloom, like a star o'er the sea;
So on her will sunshine and calmness come down,
So glory and honor her struggles shall crown.

She will rise as the metal refined by the fire,
As a spirit sore chastened, made purer and higher;
From the woes of her past will a grandeur be born,
As the tears of the eve make the gems of the morn!

LINES OF LIFE.

IT was not smooth—the path that God
    Appointed unto me;
Nor always pleasant—but it led
    Where He would have me be.
And if I felt alone the thorns,
    And failed the flowers to greet,
It was because I *would* not see
    The blossoms at my feet.

The cup presented to my lips,—
    The cup designed for all—
Most strangely, skilfully was mixed
    With honey and with gall.
And though my tongue no sweet could taste,
    My heart no good could guess,
Yet now I know that strength was hid
    Within its bitterness.

Nor was it only light that fell
    Across my onward path;

But darkness deep, that seemed to me
　　A harbinger of wrath.
Yet over all this truth still shone
　　Like silvery lining clear,
That only in a cloud can God
　　To fallen man draw near.

Thus thorn and flower, bitter and sweet,
　　Glad sunshine and dark shade,
With skilful weavings in and out,
　　A checkered life have made.
Only the taught of God may see
　　How evenly they blend,
And the Divine, the glorious plan,
　　Begin to comprehend.

Then, looking back on what has been,
　　Or on to what may be,
Be still, my heart, and calmly wait
　　The blessed whole to see.
And may this lowly, humbling thought
　　Bid every murmur flee,—
The good is more, the evil less
　　Than is deserved by me.

"THY WILL BE DONE."

WHEN all my days were bright, and life
    With radiant joy and hope was rife;
And all I asked, and all I sought,
As if on angel wing was brought:
How easy then Thy power to own,
And cheerful say, "Thy will be done."

But when Thy hand pressed on me sore,
With weight I never felt before;
When sorrow and affliction came,
And death brought in a fearful claim,
And took my best and dearest one,
I could not say, "Thy will be done."

'Tis hard to think that good can spring
From such an evil, bitter thing;
'Tis hard to think that it can be
The hand of *Love* thus laid on me;
And hard to see my hopes o'erthrown,
And yet to say, "Thy will be done."

Thy heavenly grace Thou must impart,
Thy Spirit breath upon this heart,
And every quivering pulse must thrill
With Thy soft whisper, " Peace, be still,"
Ere I can turn each weary moan
Into the words, " Thy will be done."

I can but bring to Thee my grief,
And cry, "Lord, help my unbelief!"
I can but at Thy footstool stay,
Till Thou shalt teach my heart to say,
With upward glance and childlike tone,
And patient trust, " Thy will be done."

HE LEADETH ME.

Psalm xxiii. 2.

SOMETIMES through pleasant shades,
   By softly murmuring streams;
Along sweet-scented glades,
   Lighted by golden beams:
And He who walks beside me there,
Makes all its loveliness more fair.

Sometimes o'er thorny ways,
   That wound and pierce my feet;
And danger 'round me plays,
   And tempests o'er me beat:
Though never path so dark and dread,
I do but follow in His tread.

Sometimes through blazing fires
   That singe, and scorch, and burn,
Lifting their lurid spires
   Whichever way I turn:

Yet through the hottest flames I see
The same dear Hand that leadeth me.

Sometimes through raging streams,
    That lash, and fright, and chill;
Where echo wakes wild screams,
    That numbing senses thrill:
Yet is He ever at my side
Whose voice can still the raging tide.

He leads, whose tender love
    My yearning heart enfolds;
He guides, who leads above,
    And as He guides, upholds:
I follow—though I see no more
Than one short footstep just before.

He leads, who ruleth all:
    He guides, who never errs:
With Him, how can I fall?
    Or how give place to fears?
All faith in self for ever gone,
I trust in Him, and am led on.

MY SAVIOUR.

EARTHLY friends with bliss surround me,
  Love's own air I gently breathe;
Beauties new, above, around me,
  Their beguiling witcheries wreathe;
      But their temptings,
      Sweet, soft temptings,
On me vainly, coldly fall;
      For my Saviour,
      My own Saviour,
Is more fair, more dear than all.

They can bitterly deceive me,
  They can promise and not give;
In my darkest hours they leave me,
  Hopelessly alone to grieve;
      In my sorrow,
      Pain and sorrow,

They have naught that can avail;
     But my Saviour,
     My strong Saviour,
Cannot leave me, cannot fail.

He is all my joy, my pleasure,
     All my might, my hope, my trust;
Here my soul's abiding treasure,
     Firm and faithful, true and just;
          In the future,
          Dim, dark future,
He is all the light I see;
          O my Saviour,
          My dear Saviour,
Heaven is nothing without Thee!

When I see my strength departing,
     Like the early morning dew;
Waves of anguish o'er me starting,
     And earth gliding from my view;
          No cold doubting,
          Fear or doubting,

Then shall dim my closing eye;
On my Saviour,
My dear Saviour,
I will calmly rest and die.

In the world of bliss above me,
With unending joys in store;
With the spirits pure that love me,
And the selfsame Lord adore,
There in safety,
Rest and safety,
From all sin, all sorrow free,
O my Saviour,
My dear Saviour,
May I ever live with Thee!

COME UNTO ME.

St. Matthew xi. 28.

ART thou weary? Wouldst thou rest?
Come, and lean upon this breast;
Come, and find a place with Me,
Long ago prepared for thee.

Art thou thirsty? From the brink
Of destruction turn, and drink
Of the water I will give,
And thou shalt for ever live.

Art thou on doubt's billows toss'd,
All thy charts, thy reckoning lost?
Come, to Me thy woes confide;
Come, and I will be thy Guide.

Dost thou fear the chilling breath
Of the mighty conqueror, Death?
Come, with Me there is no strife;
Come, I am eternal life.

Come, I long have sought for thee;
Come, unending bliss foresee;
Come, thy highest powers employ,
Come, and fill the heavens with joy.

OUR CUP AND BAPTISM.

*" Ye shall drink indeed of My cup, and be baptized with the baptism
I am baptized with."—St. Matthew xx. 23.*

WE dream of the triumph, we speak of the crown,
　　We look for the harvest, we long to lie down
With the martyrs and saints who have passed on be-
　　fore,
And are safe with their palms on the " bright, shining
　　shore."

We forget the long labor, the race, and the cross,
The hungerings, the thirstings, the wanderings, the
　　loss;
We forget the stern charge when He marshalled us
　　forth,
And we ask our reward and our rest upon earth.

But He told us, " The cup that I drink ye must drain;
Ye must taste of the anguish, the bitter, the pain;

Ye have asked in My might and My glory to share,
But My sorrow, and suffering, and shame, can ye
    bear?"

Oh! measure the distance, weigh justly the cost;
Go over the reckoning, or all may be lost;
For the scourge must be felt, and the cross must be
    borne,
Ere the throne can be gained, or the crown can be
    worn.

He told us of treasures, of blessings, of gains,
And He told of bereavements, of struggles, and pains;
He spake of a rest, and a comfort in store;
But the rest is to come when the conflict is o'er.

Then more of the cross, and less of the crown!
Long more for the struggle, and less to lie down;
Not always the rest and the end are in view,
But He who hath promised is faithful and true!

THE WORD OF GOD.

" Thy word have I hid in my heart."— *Psalm* cxix. 11.
" How sweet are Thy words."—*Psalm* cxix. 103.

ONE word of my God in the morning,
     When the labors of life must be done;
One strong, quickening word of the Father,
     That my spirit may feed upon.
Let me hear then the voice that sayeth,
     "This is the path and the way;"
Let me see the clear light that shineth
     Brighter and brighter each day:
That my feet may not stumble or falter
     In pathways untried and untrod,
And my soul go forth to the conflict
     Equipped with the armor of God.

One word of my God in the noon-day;
     When, weary of struggling with sin,
The shield of my faith is all tarnished,
     And my spirit is fainting within.

8

Let me hear that Jehovah still reigneth
    Unchanged and unchanging above;
And no power that darkness engenders,
    His throne eternal can move:
That my faith and my hope may be brightened,
    And my spirit again grow strong
In the thought of the patient long-suffering
    Of God, that alloweth the wrong.

One word of my God in the evening:
    Ere forgetfulness steal o'er my frame,
Let the day's last whispering echo
    The One, Omnipotent Name.
Let me read of the beautiful city,
    Of the rest that remaineth above,
When my soul, like a child that is weary,
    Is yearning for comfort and love:
That my sleep may be deeper and sweeter
    For thought of the fadeless and fair:
And my dreams may be of the mansions
    That Jesus hath gone to prepare.

COMFORTABLE WORDS.

" Comfort ye, comfort ye, My people."—*Isaiah* xl. 1.

PILGRIM, weary and oppressed,
    Dost thou seek and sigh for rest?
Is thy pathway long and drear;
Full of danger, void of cheer?
Rough and thorny though it be,
Know it is the best for thee.

Not by fortune, not by chance,
Not by human vigilance,
Were the windings of one hour
Marked by earthly wisdom's power.
All was drawn and traced above
By the heart and hand of Love.

Just the station, good or ill,
Thou, and thou alone, canst fill;
Just the sorrow, just the care,
Just the pleasure thou canst bear;
Just heaven's vast and wise design,
Sad and murmuring soul, is thine.

Not some great, some mighty task,
Does thy patient Saviour ask;
Kindly, gently, doth He bear
With thy weakness, with thy fear;
Little things He gives to thee,
Faithful in that little be.

In thy sufferings meekly borne,
In reproach, contempt, and scorn:
In the humble round of life
Spreading peace, and stilling strife;
In each thought, and deed, and word,
Thou may'st glorify thy Lord.

He hath given to thee a place;
See thou fillest it with grace;
He hath portioned out thy tasks;
Patient faithfulness He asks:
Daily by hope's cheering beam
Thou may'st bear and work with Him.

Work with Him!—transporting thought!—
Work with Him who wonders wrought!

COMFORTABLE WORDS.

Him whose power all time transcends;
Him to whom creation bends;
Work with Him to share above
In His glory, grace, and love.

Weary! there is yet a rest,
Deep, unbroken, perfect, blest!
Mourner! there is joy for thee
Where no grief, no pain can be!
To the faithful shall be given
Rest, and joy, and peace—in heaven!

WHAT I BELIEVE.

"Fear not; only believe."—*St. Mark* v. 36.

I DO believe that Jesus did
    Himself an offering give,
That fully, freely pardoned, I
    Eternally might live.

I do believe that He can take
    This tainted heart of sin,
And purify and make it fit
    For Him to dwell within.

I do believe that Jesus hears
    My every prayer and plea;
And measures not His gifts by what
    My poor, weak faith may be.

I do believe that life, nor death,
    Nor any other thing,
Can separate me from the love
    Of Christ, my Saviour King.

I do believe that He hath gone
 A mansion to prepare,
Within His Father's house, and He
 Will come and take me there.

I do believe if I endure
 With patience to the end,
Resisting unto death, that He
 Will sure deliverance send.

I do believe that as He rose,
 The first-fruits of the dead,
So from the grave I too shall rise
 To Christ, my living Head.

I do believe I shall the King
 In all His beauty see;
And that where'er my Saviour is
 I shall for ever be!

IN SICKNESS.

I ASK not why in God's decree
This weary sickness comes to me:
Why days of pain and nights of woe
With laggard footsteps come and go.

Whether it be to try my faith
And patience in His seeming wrath;
Or to correct some ill in me
Only the eye of heaven can see,

I may not tell; but this I know,
'Tis God who thus hath laid me low;
God—who hath measured out our days,
God—just and good in all His ways.

The Father chasteneth whom He loves,
And in His chastening pity moves;
'Tis for our endless good; that we
Sharers of cross and crown may be.

No greater comfort can we know
Than thus to be like Christ below;
Suffering with Him; like Him to rise
Through suffering perfect to the skies.

Father, I take it. 'Tis from Thee;
Mingled, like all Thy gifts to me;
And if no thanks my lips unclose,
My heart Thy tender pity knows.

Oh! let me, bending to Thy will,
And trusting Thy great love, lie still:
So shall these painful moments be
Strong cords to draw me nearer Thee.

THE WORKMAN AND THE METAL.

"The workman sits at the door of his furnace, watching the metal within. When he sees his own image reflected from the molten metal, he knows the process is successful, and abates the fury of the flames.

THE workman lights his glowing fire,
　　And puts the ore within the blaze,
And sits beside the furnace door,
And turns the metal o'er and o'er;
And when in it his eye can trace
The clear reflection of his face,
He knows it pure, and then allays
The fierceness of the burning rays.

So Jesus lights His glowing fire,
　　And puts the soul within the blaze;
And then beside the furnace door
He sits and turns it o'er and o'er;
And when He sees reflected there
His own sweet image clear and fair,
He knows the process is complete,
And lowers the cleansing, melting heat.

O Jesus, hotly glows the fire!
   I know Thy breath hath fanned the blaze;
I know Thou art beside the door,
Looking my spirit o'er and o'er;
Withdraw not Thou the burning heat
Until the process is complete,
Till every eye in me may trace
The bright reflection of Thy face.

THE PROMISES OF GOD.

LIKE the lovely flowers of spring time, gemming
    earth's soft velvet sod,
Gently breathing full, rich fragrance, come the pro-
    mises of God.

Like stars within the firmament, lighting life's long
    night of sorrow
With their pure and steady lustre, leading on the
    glad to-morrow.

Like the cool, soft breath of evening, when the heated
    day is done,
Whispering of the rest that cometh when our race
    of life is run.

Like dewdrops fresh and cooling on the blighted,
    withered plain,
Bringing with their liquid touch a living freshness
    back again.

Like a cordial to the fainting, like a staff unto the
    weary,
Like struggling sunbeams stealing through a prison
    damp and dreary.

Like all the blessings sent by heaven wherever man
    hath trod;
Rich, full, and bounteous—open to all—blest pro-
    mises of God!

Hands they are stretched out to help us; voices clear
    and sweet that call us;
Rocks on which our feet may safely step, though
    hideous depths appal us.

Suns they are that light and cheer us all life's long
    and cloudy day;
Mile-stones that careful, loving hands have placed
    along our way.

Cool and quiet streamlets flowing from the fountains
    of the blest;
Green and tranquil islets where the soul may pause
    awhile and rest.

Purer than the pearly dewdrops, fresher than the
    breath of morning;
Sweeter than the scent of flowerets earth's jewelled
    form adorning.

Softer than the airs of summer, brighter than the
    stars of heaven;
Richer than the golden, gorgeous hues that drape
    the couch of even.

Breathing health, and strength, and freshness, as our
    onward path we plod;
Full of joy, and hope, and gladness, come the pro-
    mises of God.

Bless'd be He who hath not left us without comfort,
    without hope,
But hath sent His bright-winged promises, wide, gen-
    erous doors to ope.

The holy, glorious promises, raising guilt-stained souls
    from earth;
Quickening every palsying nerve, giving sweetest
    comfort birth.

Lifting up the fainting spirit, throwing heavenly air
and breath;
Healing every wound and sorrow, lighting e'en the
vale of death.

As God, eternal, perfect, true, deep, fathomless, and
broad,
For ever sure,—for ever ours,—bless'd promises of
God!

TRUST.

AS the tender parent heareth,
  Though his hand no gift doth bring,
When his wayward children, crying,
  Ask some pleasant, harmful thing:
So our loving heavenly Father
  Sees and hears, but answers not,
When His wayward children, crying,
  Ask some harmful thing, or lot.

As the best and happiest children
  Still their bitter cries and woes,
In the thought so calming, sheltering,
  "Father gives not—Father knows:"—
So the patient, faithful Christian
  Calms the struggle in his breast,
And his cross and station beareth,
  With "Our Father knoweth best."

H E A V E N.

THERE'S a city above with its pearly gates,
  Its walls of jasper, and streets of gold;
Its great white throne, its river of life,
  And mansions whose glories can never be told.
To the faithful of earth, that city is given;—
But city, and mansion, and throne are not heaven.

There are soft, cooling shades, there are pastures and
    streams,
  There are airs that breathe but perfume and life;
There's a glory of light that unfadingly gleams,
  And echoes that whisper of peace—not strife:
Where never a cloud o'er the brightness is driven,—
But pastures, and light, and streams are not heaven.

There are angels that stand in the presence of God;
  There are prophets who spake as the Spirit gave
    word;
There are martyrs who sealed their faith with their
    blood,
  And saints who rejoiced on earth in the Lord.

All spotless they stand, all washed and forgiven,
But angels, and prophets, and saints are not heaven.

There are songs whose melody never shall end;
　　There are crowns that neither press heavy, nor fade;
There are harps whose tones all fancy transcend,
　　And joys that never a grief can invade;
There's a rapture from which every sorrow is driven,
But anthems, and harps, and crowns are not heaven.

All glorious, and perfect, and pure as they are,
　　They still not the spirit, they fill not the heart:
Still higher it seeks its life-giving air,
　　Still struggles and sighs for a nobler part.
Oh! something more than these must be given,
Ere the raptured soul exults in its heaven.

For what are the cities, the pastures, and streams,
　　The angels, the prophets, the crowns, and the
　　　　songs?
What is the joy, the radiance that gleams
　　Eternal and pure o'er the numberless throngs?
Glorious, and perfect, and fadeless, and fair,
What are they all if Christ be not there?

Where the presence of God eternally dwells,

    And the Saviour that loved us is seen and known;

Where the glory that gleams, and the rapture that
    swells,

    Are the joys that flow from His favor alone:—

Where the smile of Jehovah to each one is given,

Where Father, Son, Spirit are, there is our heaven!

DOUBT AND FAITH.

DOUBT is the nerveless arm that hangs and
     quakes;
Faith is the hand that reaches forth and takes.

Doubt is the mist that earth and heaven can shroud;
Faith is the undimmed sun above the cloud.

Doubt is the silent, fearing to begin;
Faith, the importunate, whose pleadings win.

Doubt is the pendant, swaying to and fro;
Faith is the needle, our lost path to show.

Doubt is the rebel who dishonors God;
Faith is the subject, yielding to His rod.

Doubt is the raw recruit, who shrinks with fright;
Faith is the long-tried warrior, strong to fight.

Doubt asks " How can I know my prayers are heard !"
And Faith replies, " I trust His gracious word."

Doubt says, " The promise is too good for me;"
Faith answers, " Gifts of kings should kingly be."

Doubt says, " He lays my honor in the dust;"
And Faith, " Though he should slay, yet will I trust."

Doubt moans, " I strive with tears, but sins abound;"
Faith says, " In Christ my righteousness is found."

Doubt fixes on the earth his downcast eye ;
Faith lifts her clear and steadfast gaze on high.

Doubt haunts the darkened borders of despair ;
Faith soars to regions lofty, pure, and fair.

Doubt is of troubled and unquiet mien ;
But Faith is steadfast, tranquil, and serene

Doubt is of earth, and with the earth must die;
But Faith shall live, where now she points, on high.

O Lord, this blinding, clogging, deadening doubt,
As thou of old the demons did, cast out;

And let me pray along life's varied path,
As Thy disciples, " Lord, increase my faith."

PRESSING ONWARD.

"I press toward the mark for the prize of the high calling of God in Christ Jesus."—*Philippians* iii. 14.

ON, on, I press toward the mark,
    On, at the call of God;
On, through the rough, but heavenward paths
    By holy footsteps trod.
I hear the words, "If thou endure,"
    I feel the shock of strife;
And see clear shining overhead
    The prize eternal life.

The fainting heart may sigh for rest,
    The feet refuse to run;
Home, kindred, country, fade behind,
    And still the cry is "On!"
On, through the flying, whirling days
    Of labor, care, and gain;
On, through the laggard, weary hours
    Of suffering and pain.

On, through the beams of faith and hope,
    On, through despair and fears;
On, through the light and smiles of joy,
    On, through the mists of tears.
On, with the higher, holier zeal
    That dares to live and strive;
On, till the Judge upon the throne
    His blest " Well done!" shall give.

On, though the world may call me back,
    On, though the way be long;
The prize to him who runneth well,—
    The battle to the strong.
Who falls, but him who looks not up?
    Who faints, but first lies down?
Not *one*, but *all* may win the race,
    May wear the victor's crown.

Since time began, till time shall end,
    The tramp of march goes on;
The thousand paths the thousand tread
    Will meet at last in one.

One just Awarder of the prize
   To him that runneth given;
One race, one struggle, and one goal,
   One God, one home, one heaven!

THE SAVIOUR FOR ME.

THEY tell me the Saviour is near me,
　　Near me, and ready to aid;
That He bends from His mansion to hear me,
　　Never to scorn or upbraid;
But surely my eyes with tears must be dim;—
They have sought, but alas! have found not Him.

They tell me He speaks to His chosen
　　In accents loving and sweet,
That soften the heart almost frozen,
　　Till she rises her Master to greet.
Ah, me! that my ear is too heavy to hear
A speaker so gentle, so mighty, and near.

They tell me He smiles on the holy,
　　And comforts the mourning in heart;
That He dwells with the humble and lowly,
　　His blessing, His peace to impart;
But I am not holy, nor humble, nor meek,
Only weary and lonely,—for such would He seek?

They tell me the Saviour descended
    To ransom the sinful and lost;
  And that guilt, though deep and extended,
    His mercy can never exhaust.
The dullness and dimness are gone;—I can see
The Saviour of sinners, the Saviour for me!

FISHERS' EVENING SONG.

On the shores of the Adriatic Sea it is customary for the wives of
the fishermen to come down about sunset, and sing a melody. After
singing the first stanza they listen awhile for the answering strain off
the water, and continue to sing and listen till well known voices come
borne on the tide, telling them that their loved ones are almost home.

WHEN sunset floods with amber hue
  The lovely Adrian shore,
The fishers' happy wives come down,
 Singing a stanza o'er;
And listening till across the main
Is borne to them an answering strain.

How sweetly to the fisherman,
 Fainting with toil, must come
At eve those dear familiar notes
 From the loved ones at home!
How strong they make his weary hand,
Striving to reach the distant land!

And thus in life's still eventide
　　The blessed spirits come,
Singing to us angelic songs,
　　Singing of rest and home;
A id listening at the golden gate,
They for the faint earth-echoes wait.

And thus do weary, toiling ones,
　　Their hours of labor o'er,
At even turn their longing eyes
　　Towards the shining shore;
Thus hear familiar voices come,
Welcoming them to heaven and home.

JESUS.

I LOVE to read of Jesus,
　　Of all He said and taught,
And of the mighty wonders
　　He on the earth hath wrought.
No story wild and thrilling
　　By lip of mortal told,
Hath ever moved my spirit
　　Like that sweet tale of old.

I love to think of Jesus,
　　The true and steadfast Friend,
Whose love so deep and wondrous
　　Can never change or end.
It warms my faith to action,
　　It bids my fears depart;
It stays my fainting spirit,
　　And rests my weary heart.

I love to talk of Jesus
  With those who know Him well;
And of His sweet compassion
  In holy converse tell.
To find how very many
  Adore and love my Lord;
And how His grace unfailing
  Comfort and strength afford.

I love to work for Jesus;
  To feel that all I do
Is for the heavenly Master,
  Who asks a service true.
My hardest toil is nothing
  To what He did for me;
Oh! may I ne'er grow weary
  Of working, Lord, for Thee!

I soon shall be with Jesus,
  Who sits enthroned above;
I soon shall be with Jesus,
  Whom here, unseen, I love.

And oh! the thought that maketh
　The spirit world so fair,
And floods it o'er with glory,
　Is—Jesus will be there!

GOD KNOWETH BEST.

HE took them from me, one by one,
⠀⠀The things I set my heart upon;
They looked so harmless, fair, and blest;—
Would they have hurt me?—God knows best.
He loves me so He would not wrest
Them from me if it were not best.

He took them from me, one by one,
The friends I set my heart upon.
Oh! did they come,—they and their love,—
Between me and my Lord above?
Were they as idols in my breast?
It may be;—God in heaven knows best.

I will not say I did not weep,
As doth a child that longs to keep
The pleasant things in hurtful play
His wiser parent takes away;
But in this comfort I will rest—
He who hath taken knoweth best.

WORK WHILE IT IS TO·DAY.

WORK while it is to-day;
    The hour will pass away;
Another's hand will do
What was designed for you;
Another's crown will bear
The star *you* ought to wear.

Work while it is to-day;
The need will pass away;
The heart that you might soothe,
The path that you might smooth,
The soul you might beseech,
Will be beyond your reach.

Work while it is to-day;
 You soon will pass away
Where neither strength nor skill
Can any work fulfil;
Or suffering atone
For that here left undone.

OUR GIFTS.

DOES God need aught from us that we should make
  Of our poor gifts to Him an offering?
We add not to His store,—yet doth He look
  With eye of tenderness on what we bring,
As parents from their children trifles take,
And hold them ever dear for love's sweet sake.

I think God's treasuries, where He doth keep
  The gifts His children here have brought to Him,
Will be like many a mother's secret store
  Of relics of her offspring—worn and dim,—
Full of the things no other heart but hers
Would count of value, or look on with tears.

We shall not know them after He hath priced
  Them; as the gentle Mary did not know
What her anointing was. Within His hands
  Our worthless gifts with heavenly lustre glow,—
More precious in His eyes than gold or gem,
For sake of love that He can see in them.

THY TROUBLE.

THY trouble, whatsoe'er it be,
 Know God hath bound it upon thee,
By special Providence to prove
And try thy constancy and love;
With kindest purpose to reward
And crown thee as thy faithful Lord.

The cords that bind thou canst not break,
And struggling doth them tighter make;
Therefore lie gently down, and take
What God designs for thy own sake;
And suffer thou His hand to do
As pleaseth Him, the Wise and True.

Thou canst not see nor understand
The mystic working of His hand;
Thou knowest not what ills His love
Doth painfully from thee remove,
Nor how His purposes can be
In any way fulfilled in thee.

So count not thou thy Lord unjust,
But hold thee still; believe and trust;
Thou hast, to hush each spirit-wail,
The promise that can never fail;
Thou hast the word of God to tell
That. in the end it shall be well!

THE DEAD IN CHRIST.

OH! call them not dead—they are not now sleeping
    In the cold earth where we laid them to rest;
But while o'er their ashes we bend, fondly weeping,
    They smile on our tears from the homes of the blest.

They toiled once below as we are now toiling,
    They suffered and wept as their crosses they bore;
But now where no tempter may ever come spoiling,
    They rest where they suffer—they sorrow no more.

Not alone in our anguish and grief have they left us
    To struggle with dangers that compass us here;
But through the hot trials that mould us and sift us
    They utter sweet whispers of comfort and cheer.

ST. JAMES' CHURCH.*

I LOVE this church!—I love to sit
 Within this hallowed place;
The air, the books, the very walls,
 My flagging spirits brace.
I love to leave the world without,
 With every care and fear,
And come in earnest, childlike trust,
 To feel that God is here.

Oh! 'mid the vexing scenes of life,
 Its anxious toil and care,
How often have I sought this house
 In earnest faith and prayer!
This house—where never yet e'er came,
 In anguish and dismay,
A sorrowing heart in humble trust
 That went unblessed away.

* Warrenton, Va.

The holiest memories of my soul
   Are mingled with this place;
Nor time, nor change, nor life, nor death,
   Their record can efface.
Here, in meek worship, often bowed
   All whom my heart held dear;
And all I ever knew of good—
   Of God—was taught me here.

Here on my brow, in infancy,
   The cross of Christ was traced;
And on my head, in after years,
   A prelate's hands were placed.
Here have I knelt in humble faith
   Before my Saviour's board,
And felt, as only here is felt,
   The pardoning peace of God.

The spirits of the sainted dead
   About this temple move,
Whose voices mingled once with mine
   In words of praise and love.

I feel that they are here to-day,
    Those unseen worshippers,
Blending the feeble songs of earth
    With heavenly choristers.

I love this church! I love her words
    Of holy prayer and praise,
That far above this world of sin
    Our fettered spirits raise.
In her the sweetest, purest joys
    That crown my life are found;
And o'er my sleeping dust her voice
    Of heavenly hope shall sound.

Church of my heart!—thy lasting peace
    Shall claim my latest breath;
And when my feeble heart and tongue
    Are cold and mute in death,—
Still may thy sacred songs be sung,
    Still may thy prayers ascend,
Until in triumph He shall come
    Whose reign shall have no end!

INFANT BAPTISM.

INTO Christ's flock we give thee now,
    Lamb of our little fold;
Into the love, the heavenly care,
    By lips of earth untold.

The blessed Arms that children took,
    The Heart that bade them come,
Are opened wide for thee to-day,
    A refuge and a home.

Into Christ's flock,—where never power
    Lamb from its Shepherd parts;
Into Christ's flock,—that blissful rest
    For weary, aching hearts!

We sign thee with His cross of love,
    We name thee with His name;
Child of His covenant of grace,
    Heir of a royal claim!

O little heart, ne'er from this fold
   Of peace and safety stray;
O little feet, though tempted oft,
   Keep in the narrow way;—

That so the life begun with sign
   Of bitterest pangs and woes,—
The life begun with *suffering* Christ
   With *reigning* Christ shall close!

ALL SAINTS' DAY.

TO our dear ones in Christ, who with
    The holy angels live
A higher, truer life than ours,
    This day of Saints we give.

Each year some home is shadowed o'er,
    Some heart in sorrow faints;
Each year adds to the shining ranks
    Of church and household saints.

Small part are we on earth of that
    Innumerable throng,
That the eternal Throne surrounds
    With full, triumphant song.

Our Saints !—whom even death from us
    But for a season parts !
We bear them in our inmost thoughts,
    We name them in our hearts !

Our Saints!—they loved us well on earth;
    And now, exalted thus,
Their faces, glorious with the light
    Of heaven, still turn to us!

Our Saints!—they have but higher gone
    At our dear Master's call;
Still members of the self-same fold,
    One God above us all!

We worship here with fettered powers,
    They with angelic might;
We in the mists and shadows grope,
    They walk in joy and light.

They are with Christ; they wait for us,
    As for expected guest,
Who may be nearer than we think
    To that sweet land of rest.

Let thoughts of them our aching hearts
    With hope and gladness fill,
And may the calm that rests on them,
    Our troubled spirits still.

Thanks for the Saints who once with us
 The narrow pathway trod!
Thanks for the tried, the faithful souls
 At rest, to-day, with God.

They perfected with us shall be,
 And one in heart and soul;
Whom death hath parted, death shall join,
 One grand, one living whole!

COMMUNION THOUGHTS.

BEFORE COMMUNION.

SAVIOUR, I hear Thy loving voice
  Bidding me come to Thee;
I see Thy board before me spread
  With mercy wide and free.

Unworthy to pick up the crumbs
  That from Thy table fall,
My guilty soul would shrink away
  But for Thy pleading call.

I dare not slight that gracious voice,—
  I dare not turn away,
While Mercy stands with open arms,
  And Jesus bids me stay.

Forgetting all but Thy own words,
   I, trembling, come to Thee;
No other plea upon my lips
   But—Thou hast died for me.

Oh! may Thy kind, forgiving love
   My heavenly portion be;
Pardon, and strength, and peace I need,
   And they are found in Thee.

THE INVITATION.

"Draw near with faith, and take this holy sacrament to your comfort."—*Prayer Book.*

DRAW near with faith.   Behold, the Saviour stands
With tender, yearning heart, and outstretched hands;
With pleading voice He meekly deigns to crave,
Ready to hear, to pity, and to save.

Draw near with faith.   Leave all thy doubts behind;
Distrust Him not who is so true and kind.
Draw near, and see thy timid fears grow less;
He greets with love;—He only waits to bless.

Draw near with faith.   Unworthy though thou art,
Offer to Him—'tis all He asks—thy heart.
Not here He stands to call the righteous home;
He calls the sinner—as a sinner come.

10

Come with repentance, earnest, deep, and true,
With love for Him to whom all love is due;
Forgiving as thou art of God forgiven,
At peace with men, with conscience, and with heaven.

Draw near with faith.   Bring all thy heavy care;
Thou hast no load thy Saviour will not bear;
He knows thy grief, He feels thy bitterest woe;
Himself hath walked the weary path below.

Draw near with faith.   Dost thou not sorely need
Comfort and strength thy drooping soul to speed?
Draw near and feel how true, how strong his heart,
And find the power He only can impart.

Draw near with faith.   Oh! can that voice of love
One cold or careless spirit fail to move?
Turn not away; this pleading call may be
The last thou canst reject,—the last for thee!

AFTER COMMUNION.

ALL glory be to Thee, Most High,
   Most Wonderful and Good,
That Thou hast given for love of me
   Thy body and Thy blood.

O Love that gave, that bore so much,
   O Love, so vast and deep,
Safely within Thy sheltering folds
   My wandering spirit keep.

For I am Thine,—called by Thy name,—
   Thy seal is on my brow;
Angels and men have witnessed here
   My world-renouncing vow.

Oh! may this bread and wine of life
   So fill my soul and heart,
I ne'er will seek for other food,
   Will ne'er from Thee depart.

Each day to me this feast renew,
  And keep me one in Thee;
That I henceforth in Thee may live,
  And Thou may'st dwell in me.

DEPARTED SAINTS.

'We also bless Thy Holy Name for all Thy servants departed this life in Thy faith and fear; beseeching Thee to give us grace so to follow their good examples, that with them we may be partakers of Thy heavenly kingdom.''— *Prayer Book*.

WE bless Thee for the holy ones departed,
    The good of every land, and age, and clime;
The meek, the constant, and the noble-hearted,
    Whose glorious deeds illume the shores of time,
And life's high paths and noble aims revealing,
For God and Truth shall never cease appealing.

In bitter grief a heavy cross they carried,
    And blood and tears their weary steps bedewed;
And oft they sank while their Deliverer tarried,
    Yet at His word, refreshed and unsubdued,
They fearless met each hellish foe assailing,
And faithful stood, with Christ the Lord prevailing,

They lived to earth a very scorn and wonder,
    Afflicted and tormented, tortured, slain;

Were mocked and scourged, were stoned and sawn
    asunder,
  Were tried and tempted, bound with bond and
    chain;
Forsaken, homeless,—yet with songs ascending
The heavenly court, whose glories know no ending.

We bless Thee that the world has seen such holy,
  Such hearts that never swerved from truth and
    Thee;
But with a faith undaunted and yet lowly,
  Served Thee through blood, fire, death, and infamy,
That she may know there are who faithful bearing
Their cross on earth, their crowns in heaven are
    wearing.

We bless Thee for the saintly ones among us,
  Whom we have loved, and mourned, and laid to
    rest;
Whose parting words with quivering anguish wrung
    us,
  Though breathed upon the threshold of the blest;
Whose fair examples shining ever o'er us
Make bright the paths their footsteps pressed before
    us.

We bless Thee, though the bitter tears are falling,
    Though lone our hearts, and sad our firesides be;
Though for them still our yearning souls are calling,
    We bless Thee that they are at rest with Thee,
Where everlasting joys and pleasures centre,
And never pain, nor sin, nor death, may enter.

We bless Thee that Thou once didst lend them to us,
    The precious jewels Thou wilt keep and wear;
We bless Thee that familiar voices woo us
    To the blest land where all our treasures are;
And when we reach that shore, loved forms will
      meet us,
And hearts that we have known and missed will greet
      us.

Lord, give us grace their shining steps to follow,
    To live and die as they have lived and died;
In, but not of, a world false-hearted, hollow,
    Seeking above our Saviour, Friend, and Guide;
And faithful to the end to Thee, the Giver,
Sit down with them at Thy blest board 'for ever!

Milton Keynes UK
Ingram Content Group UK Ltd.
UKHW041810080224
437337UK00027B/70